Advance praise for
MY BRIGHT MIDNIGHT

"*My Bright Midnight* is a wonderfully engrossing tale that packs in romance, friendship, family, murder, and a dash of crime, all lovingly set against the colorful backdrop of New Orleans. But the true star here is Josh Russell's clean and elegant prose, and how truly he renders the voice of his main character, Walter, a German immigrant haunted by his dark past while trying to earn a place for himself in America. I ended up reading this book in one day—pick it up and you won't be able to put it down."—**Hannah Tinti, author of** *The Good Thief*

♦ ♦ ♦

"I've been waiting for more of Josh Russell's NOLA since *Yellow Jack,* waiting patiently, most of the time, and now it's paid off. This book flat out kicks ass in its New Orleansness but also in its humanness, a novel firing on all cylinders, amazing characters, killer details, lyrical language, and a plot that keeps the pages turning. A book worth the wait and worth its salt, a novel to read and reread, to savor, to treasure."—**Tom Franklin, author of** *Hell at the Breech* **and** *Crooked Letter, Crooked Letter*

♦ ♦ ♦

"Josh Russell anchors *My Bright Midnight,* his wonderfully paced second novel, with two memorable, sensual characterizations—one of them, Nadine, the book's heroine; the other, a city, New Orleans. Between the two, Russell fashions a most rare feat: that of a fresh love story."—**Stuart Dybek, author of** *I Sailed with Magellan*

"In Josh Russell's neo-realistic, hyper historical novel *My Bright Midnight*, we are given a panoramic view of home front New Orleans that is, at once, sweeping and swept, fat and lean in the extreme. It is a map more detailed than the thing it represents, defamiliarizing both ways—making the ordinary awfully wonderful and the wonderful as normal as hell, as heaven. It is a remarkable achievement of exaggerated understatement. A book translated from the native tongue of fevered dreams and dreamy fevers."—**Michael Martone, author of *Racing in Place: Collages, Fragments, Postcards, Ruins***

MY BRIGHT MIDNIGHT

YELLOW SHOE FICTION

Michael Griffith, Series Editor

LOUISIANA STATE UNIVERSITY PRESS)(BATON ROUGE

MY BRIGHT
MIDNIGHT

a novel

JOSH RUSSELL

Published by Louisiana State University Press
Copyright © 2010 by Josh Russell
All rights reserved
Manufactured in the United States of America
LSU Press Paperback Original
First printing

Designer: Michelle A. Neustrom
Typefaces: Whitman, text; Futura, display
Printer and binder: Thomson-Shore, Inc.

Library of Congress Cataloging-in-Publication Data
Russell, Josh.
My bright midnight : a novel / Josh Russell.
p. cm. — (Yellow shoe fiction)
ISBN 978-0-8071-3696-6 (pbk. : alk. paper)
I. Title.
PS3568.U76677M9 2010
813'.54—dc22

2010008643

For Kathryn,
who was there at the beginning,

and Lola,
who showed up at the end

Kath, every word of this book is for you.

Thank you, Michael Griffith, for twenty years of friendship and good advice; thank you, Nicola Mason, for your wise eyes and kind reassurances; thank you, Michael Koch, for asking so many times, "Got anything interesting?" and for the kindness of publishing several sections of *My Bright Midnight* in *Epoch;* thank you, David Racine and Wayne Wilson and Peter Rock and Tim Parrish and Joshua Harmon, for listening to me complain (the sincerest form of brotherhood); thank you, Joe DeSalvo, for telling me about seeing POWs in New Orleans; thank you, Lee Campbell Sioles and Michelle Neustrom and Eizabeth Gratch, for your patience and wisdom and gimlet eyes; and thank you, John Easterly, for making sure everything went smoothly.

A Georgia State University Summer Research Enhancement Grant and a National Endowment for the Arts Literature Fellowship provided me with invaluable support.

MY BRIGHT MIDNIGHT

◆◆◆

My cousin and I were born a few weeks apart in 1910, Andreas first, and we were together every day as we grew up in Munich. When we were four years old, our fathers went away to war together. Neither came back. We were matching orphans in patched pants. Then my aunt gave in to loneliness and married a man named Moser, a man from our neighborhood who claimed he'd seen our fathers killed by Americans who'd lured them into no-man's-land to trade wine for tobacco. Overnight, Andreas had a new surname, a new father, new clothes. I envied my cousin's good fortune and hated my mother's loyalty: Moser had come to her first and proposed marriage, but she sent him away. Andreas caught beetles and flies with a butterfly net and identified them with leather-bound entomology guides while my mother and I ate stale bread and lived in two cold rooms with a hall toilet.

One day in the park while we were hunting bugs, Andreas said I was no longer good enough to be his cousin because Moser had called me a bastard and my mother a prostitute. When he turned his back to me, I hooked my arm around his neck and choked him until he fell to his knees. I rode him down while he gagged and clawed at my elbow. "I'll kill you," I told him calmly, tightening my hold, and he stopped struggling. "*You're* the bastard. *Your* mother's the whore." He nodded against my arm and then stopped moving. For a long moment I pretended I'd killed him, then I got scared, and when I let him go he fell weeping into the turned dirt of a flowerbed.

1

I told my mother what he'd said—I was eight years old and couldn't keep secrets—and she forbade me from speaking to him. At first it hurt me less to be alone than it did to see Andreas' toys. Soon, however, I missed my cousin more than I missed my father. I knew there was no chance I'd ever see my father again, but I could walk to where Andreas lived in less than an hour.

I managed somehow to keep from my mother the secret that at least once a week I went to spy on him. Sometimes all I could do was stare at closed curtains, but often enough they were open and I could watch Andreas and my aunt and Herr Moser in their parlor, and I jealously imagined being on the other side of the glass with them, drinking tea and eating cakes. It took only a few months for me to grow bored, and though I feared this boredom might hint at a weakness within me, I stopped sneaking off to watch Andreas play his violin or read the newspaper or pick his nose.

I was sixteen when it occurred to me that my mother was sick, not just sad my father was long dead and we were poor. I was working at a bookshop, running deliveries, fetching the owner's lunch, packing and unpacking boxes, following an insulting map that directed the order the shop's five trashcans were to be emptied. Between tasks I puzzled out mysteries—Sherlock Holmes, *The Moonstone,* Agatha Christie. A few were translated into German, most were not—the bookshop was near the university and sold books in many languages. Those in English were my double puzzles, mysterious deaths wrapped inside mysterious words I learned one by one from a thick dictionary.

My mother's mystery I tried to solve by reading receipts for morphine and iron tablets and vitamins. While she slept I hunted for more clues and found a box of pictures. My mother hated to be photographed, and in every snapshot she covered her face, so it was impossible to tell when the photographs had been taken: my mother standing beside a fountain, behind a handkerchief; my

2

mother pointing at a monkey in a cage while shielding her face with her hand; my mother sitting on a step, hiding behind *The Sorrows of Young Werther.* There were pictures of my father squinting at the sun with his foot on a tree stump, grinning with his foot on a croquet ball, scowling with his foot on the step below the one on which my mother sat.

One Monday, digging in the trash for a dirty French postcard I'd pocketed at the bookshop, brought home, and then been unable to find where I thought I'd hidden it, I discovered, wadded into a ball, the draft of a letter my mother had written my aunt. It solved the riddle: A beauty spot's taproot had grown deep, and cancer was in my mother's bones and blood. I made myself angry with her for keeping the secret so that I wouldn't tell her that I knew, so that I wouldn't cry, so that I wouldn't think about what would happen to me when she died—*Perhaps Moser will take pity on him,* she'd hoped to my aunt. There was no joy in solving her mystery.

Saturday morning she was too weak to get out of bed, and when I brought her an egg and some coffee, she begged me to get her a licorice whip. "I dreamed of how you and Andreas used to make me and your Aunt Hannelore buy you candy when we walked in the park, and now I can't imagine eating anything else." When I came back, she was curled on the bedroom floor. First I thought she was asleep, but I waited for her to breathe, and she didn't. The little bottle of morphine I'd fetched from the apothecary the day before stood empty beside her untouched egg—a week of dulling doses downed in a single swallow, my mother a suicide. A scrap of the photograph of my father playing croquet was on the carpet near her mouth, and empty beside her was the box that'd held the pictures of her covering her face. She'd eaten them, I guessed, though I couldn't think why she would. I wished for a moment that she'd left me one or two, but I realized it was a selfish wish. They were her memories, not mine. I sat beside her and ate the licorice, a memory we shared.

I was eighteen before I saw my cousin again. It'd been nearly ten years since I'd peeked into his house, but I recognized his face when I saw it across a crowded Schwabing barroom. Andreas was with a short blonde who wore a tall Russian fur cap. I was going to honor my mother by snubbing him, but before I could finish my beer, Andreas had his arm around my neck and was wetly kissing my ear.

"How's Auntie?" he asked, and I thought he was being cruel.

"Two years dead," I told him, not turning my head.

"Moser is a terrible man. I had no idea," he explained when he found his voice. "Auntie's name isn't spoken in his house. My mother is his slave."

My cousin introduced the blonde—Ilse, his fiancée—and demanded I come for a drink at their flat, which turned out to be five lavishly appointed rooms overlooking Leopoldstrasse. "This is Ilse's parents'," my cousin admitted. "Her father's a professor of philosophy, and he's teaching in Frankfurt this year." In a library filled with what I recognized as rare and valuable books, we drank schnapps from cut crystal, and for a moment my childish wish was granted: I was with my cousin on the other side of the window glass.

Andreas boasted that he was studying at the university and that he and Ilse were to be married in April.

"Are you a student?" Ilse asked.

"I work in a bookshop," I said.

Their polite smiles drove me to gulp my drink and excuse myself. Walking under stars frozen in the winter sky, I imagined Andreas and Ilse in her parents' bed reading novels the way I sometimes imagined other couples I knew having animalistic sex.

Andreas and I began to meet every Friday at the barroom in Schwabing. Though my cousin admitted Moser couldn't be trusted, and had many times changed details of how our fathers had been killed, we clung to our belief that they'd been murdered by Americans. We ripped down broadsides advertising Wild West shows and American circuses, harassed tourists we heard speaking flat English, pissed on the red, white, and blue flag painted on the side of the shop that sold American whiskey and phonograph records.

I didn't mention the books I helped sell, or confess to Andreas that for years I'd been teaching myself English, first as part of an absurd plan to seek revenge, a plan that faded when I realized it was foolish to think learning their language would lead me to the men who killed my father, and then as a way to help me figure out who killed made-up men. Learning English made me feel less a failure, though I felt vaguely guilty each time I translated a line of English or formed an English word with my lips.

One drunken night, as we hunted in vain for an American flag to tear down and burn, my cousin described Ilse's naked body in detail, including a birthmark shaped like a bird and the fact that he made her shave her pubic hair. Then he listed the public places where they'd coupled: the park, the opera, the train station. I was shocked and jealous, and rather than telling him the story of my one night with the shy girl from the milliner's who'd softly cried the entire time we were in bed, I invented an elaborate narrative of my sexual conquests based on pornography I'd read in the bookshop's backroom.

Andreas tried to slap my back but was so drunk he missed, stumbled, slipped on slick cobbles, and fell flat on his face. I'd matched him drink for drink all night, and when I rolled him over I was sure he was dead; then he turned his head and puked. His nose was bloody, and he'd lost a tooth. It's a wonder I kept my feet when I slung him over my shoulder and carried him home to Ilse.

She answered the door in a nightgown that reminded me of those my mother had worn, and I felt ashamed for gawking at her breasts, though she didn't seem to notice. I laid my cousin on a couch, and she wiped his face with a cloth she fetched from the kitchen. Blood and vomit had blackened the tooth I thought he'd knocked out; his nose wasn't even swollen. Only Andreas could fall on his face and arise unmarked.

"He's drunk more nights than he's sober," Ilse complained. My cousin snored. She bent to cover him with a lap rug, and I stared at her rear end and tried to think of something besides what Andreas had told me but couldn't. I put my hand between her legs, and when she straightened and turned and slapped me, I grabbed the back of her head and pushed her mouth against mine, and with my other hand I squeezed one of the breasts my cousin had bragged of biting. She didn't struggle, and she seemed to be holding her breath. When I let her go and stepped back, she wouldn't look at me. "You're as bad as he is," she said without emotion. "Perhaps worse."

In the street I smelled my hands like a pervert and then dunked them into a greasy puddle.

For days I was haunted by visions of Ilse twisting in ecstasy, my body taking the place of my cousin's in the scenes he'd described, and by visions of what he'd do to me when she told him I'd kissed and groped her. All week I worried, and on Friday I went to the barroom, hoping for the beating that would blot out my guilty thoughts. There was no sign of him, and as I drank alone, I realized I'd hoped for a beating not just to erase the visions, but because I feared that once again he would vanish and that once again I would be left alone. Another beer, and I couldn't forgive him for abandoning me. One more, and I wished I'd torn off Ilse's nightgown and assaulted her while he snored.

Saturday morning I was delivering books when Andreas called my name. He came running across the street and I prepared for a punch, but instead of hitting me, he boasted that Ilse was pregnant. My fantasies had been so vivid and constant that I felt it might actually be true when I said, "It may be my child."

My cousin's smile twitched. "Your child?"

I told him about Ilse's bird-shaped birthmark, her shaved pubis, the way she seduced me in the park and train station. I described how it felt to hold her breast. It was a clumsy, stupid lie, save for the last detail, and that detail was more shameful than my lies, and I waited for Andreas to laugh, or punch me for repeating nearly verbatim what he'd told me, or punch me for kissing her while he lay passed out. Instead, he turned and walked away. I felt like an idiot. How hard would it have been to shake his hand, slap his back, congratulate him? To admit what I'd drunkenly done and beg him to forgive me?

I was so sure I'd lost my cousin for good this time that when I answered the door two weeks later and found Andreas standing there, I opened my arms to embrace him. He kicked me in the groin. I fell to my knees, and my cousin lifted with both hands the thick English dictionary I'd pilfered from the bookshop and slammed it down on my head. I curled into a ball while Andreas pounded my skull with the book until its binding broke and pages fluttered from its snapped spine and fell to the floor with a spooky hissing.

I felt blood in my ear. When I sobbed, "I'm sorry I kissed her," my cousin pulled me to my knees by my hair.

"She's dead," he said. "I made her go to an abortionist, and now she's dead."

I prayed he would kill me, but he didn't even hit me again.

The bookshop's owner, a timid man named Eckart, had helped raise money for the Nazis before the May election. He was a friend of Hitler's, and he sold him books, and though I once delivered a book addressed to him, I never met that terrible man. At Eckart's urging I read *Mein Kampf* and the pamphlets my boss helped print and distribute. I was unmoved by the boyish, ignorant anger and accusations with which they bubbled. After the film of the August rally in Nuremberg began to be shown in Munich, the contributions Eckart collected from workingmen and clerks grew from a few coins to envelopes of banknotes. I knew where he kept the cashbox, and on the day after Andreas told me Ilse was dead, I reasoned that stealing from hateful, stupid men was no crime. It was enough money to get me onto the first train leaving Munich toward a port, any port, enough to get me onto the first boat leaving Genoa for any port in America, the worst exile I could imagine, land of my father's murderers.

◆◆◆

In 1928 I hated America. Then I arrived in New Orleans in spring-time. My first day in the city I rode the streetcar without a fixed destination, changing lines at every transfer point and searching for signs offering a job and a place to live, signs a sailor promised I would see everywhere I looked. I was eighteen and had been in America for only a few hours; his promise seemed plausible. The car rocked like yet another boat, which was comforting, and from its window I saw, instead of signs, bushes of burning pink flowers I would later learn were azaleas. In the pure light the live oaks glowed like neon signs in the shapes of trees. The Munich March I'd left was cold and gray; New Orleans's version was warm and green. I smelled perfume coming from behind the ears and off the necks of girls and women on their way from school and shopping, a mingled fragrance of flowers and fruit. When I finally saw a placard in a window advertising a room for let, I stepped down from the car and stood below a blooming tree and realized perhaps what I'd smelled was New Orleans.

Before she would give me the key, I had to promise the landlady I would not drink beer or bootleg whiskey or keep company with loose women. I opened a window, and thick air perfumed by the flowering tree—sweet olive, the landlady told me—filled my little room at the back of the house.

I put my head on the pillow's crisp slip and closed my eyes. When I opened them, the sun was still shining, but its angle was different, and the hands of my watch didn't point to an hour that made sense—and then I realized I'd slept for nineteen hours and it was morning.

I got dressed and combed my hair and prepared to find the sign that would lead me to work, but when I came down to breakfast I discovered it was a local feast day. My landlady and her other roomer, a middle-aged librarian named Edward, were amazed I didn't know the custom and demanded I come with them. All over the city, altars to St. Joseph were spread with cakes and cookies and boiled shrimp. They were in churches, in people's homes, inside corner stores. I ate and ate until I nearly cried for joy. St. Joseph brought rain to parched Sicily, and the rain made the favas grow; at each altar I added a dried bean to my pocket change. "For luck," my landlady told me. I ate pasta with red gravy flavored with fennel, chewed a piece of St. Joseph's sandal rendered in bread. Moser was a liar, I decided once and for all. It was impossible to hate such a wonderful place. Then came summer.

I should've expected it after spring's hothouse flowers—lemon and orange blossoms, irises, roses, jasmine, magnolias bigger than my fists—but the heat was a surprise. The smells I'd mistaken for powder and toilet water were smothered by the stink of the crushed-shell gravel dumped on the street. In the sun it reeked of the lake bottom from which it had been dredged. After sweeping a grocery store, stacking boxes in a warehouse, and unloading bananas and barley from steamers like the one that'd brought me to America, I found a job working for Mr. Erickson, who sold maritime maps.

Every day at four the June sky darkened until it burst and rain ran down the windows and warped the view of Canal Street. Ten minutes later the pavement was steaming beneath blue heavens bright as the river that twisted on the maps tacked to the office walls. By the time Mr. Erickson and I left, the air was the only evidence a single drop had fallen. I could feel it sliding around my face and my hands as I walked. As the days passed, I grew used to it, and soon moving through the slippery air wasn't like swimming, but like being a fish.

The heat could not rob me of my appetite. I grew plump: roast beef sandwiches and fried potatoes and bottles of sweet, dark soda pop—Barq's, Coca-Cola, Big Shot; fried oysters, fried shrimp, fried chicken, fried fish on Fridays; black-eyed peas and thick links of spicy sausage beside turnip greens that'd been boiled with fatback; jambalaya, gumbo, muffalettas; chop suey and egg foo yung from the Chinaman's. I ate papayas and bananas and guavas and mangoes and kumquats and figs. I drank gallons of inky coffee laced with chicory and sweetened with the powdered sugar I shook off fried doughnuts. For dinner my landlady served fried eggplant smothered in red gravy, bell peppers stuffed with chop meat, artichokes stuffed with seafood and breadcrumbs. I ate it all, then somehow I found more room and kept eating—spearmint snowballs with condensed milk, Russian Cake, apple fried pies.

June's heat made it clear what I could expect from July and August, and I wished for a legal way to break my promise to my landlady and drink cold beer, then I grew desperate enough to consider flouting the law. In Munich I'd laughed at the Eighteenth Amendment to the Constitution of the United States, gangsters, and bathtub gin—yet more evidence of Americans' stupidity—but when I nervously asked Mr. Erickson if he knew where I could find a speakeasy, he laughed.

"This is New Orleans," he explained. "Nothing here changed in '20."

There was a bar on a corner a few blocks from my house, but I'd assumed it no longer served beer and liquor, no matter what its faded sign claimed. The dark room was cool and smoky. My shoulders loosened when I stepped inside. Without asking what I wanted, the bartender served me a schooner of cold blond beer. I looked for policemen in the gloom, sure I'd walked into a trap, but there were no policemen, and everyone was drinking. The barman hurried back to a huddle of men at the end of the bar and bent toward a newspaper from which one of the men read in an excited voice. The beer was bright and crisp, and I swallowed little moans of pleasure with each sip.

The bartender set a second glass of beer in front of me before I realized I'd finished the first. He danced a little jig and pointed down the bar to the clutch of dark shapes leaning over the paper. "Ruth," he said, "homer in the ninth," and when I looked confused, added, "Yankees," and when that clearly didn't help, asked, "You want red beans?"

I nodded—I was hungry. When I looked, there didn't seem to be a woman among the men reading the newspaper. "Who is this Ruth?" I asked. "Did she say that I know her?"

The men could not believe I didn't know who Babe Ruth was, could not believe I didn't know who the Yankees were, could not believe I was ignorant even of the basic rules of baseball.

"Where you stay?" one demanded.

"By the widow and the fairy," another answered for me.

They taught me the eight teams in the American League and wouldn't let me leave until I recited *Browns, Red Sox, White Sox, Athletics, Tigers, Indians, Senators, Yankees.*

My landlady the widow was sitting in the porch swing with Edward the fairy when I came up the walk.

"I have been drinking beer," I announced before she could smell the truth. I expected a tongue-lashing, to be told to pack my bag and find a new place to live.

"It *is* hot," she said.

"It is," Edward agreed.

They both sighed. I stood at the bottom of the porch stairs and wondered if I was too drunk to understand their displeasure.

"Did they feed you?" the widow asked.

"Yes. Red beans."

"Wash day," Edward said, and I parroted, "Wash day," as if I understood.

June curdled into July. After watching Mr. Erickson work with his compasses and rulers and brushes all morning, I delivered maps through the hottest hours of the day. My apprenticeship was unofficial, but I hoped my interest would convince him to teach me the trade. The maps went to import-export men in offices along Canal and Poydras, and to the captains who watched their ships loaded and unloaded at the wharves along the river: bananas and pineapples coming ashore, cotton and sugar leaving town. I memorized route maps and got to know the streetcar conductors who took me Uptown to the Henry Clay, Napoleon, and Louisiana Avenue wharves. I'd been in New Orleans almost three months, barely long enough to learn the names of the streets that ran alongside or ended at the river, and though it embarrassed me that I still spoke like a boy from Munich, by the middle of the summer I'd stopped seeing myself amid the crowds stumbling down gangplanks in their immigrants' coats, their foreigners' hats. Once a week or so I would spot Andreas dragging a battered suitcase, Ilse's ghost fearfully holding a handful of the back of his jacket, but then he would look up and ask for directions in an English bent by his Polish or Russian or Czech tongue, and Ilse's ghost would vanish, leaving behind a scared girl and a lost boy, and I would pretend I couldn't understand him and hurry off.

I ate my dinner at the widow's table, excused myself after dessert but before Edward made tea and tuned the radio to what my landlady called "the violin station." I spent my evenings in the barroom listening to Harold the bartender, Nolan, who drove a truck for the city, and Lou, who fixed cars at the Sinclair station down the block, talk about baseball. Only months before I'd hated America and everything about it, but now I was in love with New Orleans and falling in love with baseball. They taught me the names of the best players—Lou Gehrig, Babe Ruth, Ty Cobb, Goose Goslin.

On the morning of July 31 I found a woman in the office on Canal Street tearing a map in half, then in half again, then in half again. At her feet were hundreds of little maps she'd made.

"Ralph took off with that tart," she explained before I could ask what she thought she was doing.

It took me a moment to figure out who Ralph was—I never called Mr. Erickson by his first name. I hadn't known he had a wife, let alone a tart. She picked up another map and tore the Mississippi into segments of equal length.

"Am I ugly?" she asked.

I shook my head no, which was the truth. Mrs. Erickson was curvy and disheveled, the lace of her slip bright at the hem of her skirt.

"You're Walter," she said, like she was naming me, not asking. She held out the map she'd been destroying, and when I stepped to take it, she caught my tie and pulled my face to hers and kissed me.

The kiss seemed to last forever, as if we were stuck together, open-eyed and hissing through our noses, rather than kissing. Even while it went on, I knew neither of us was thinking of the other, and I knew when I broke away from the kiss I would dance back and trip and fall into the torn maps and then scramble quickly to the door, I would wander to the first transients' hotel I could find, rent a room and pay for a hot bath I'd sit in until it went as cold as a bath can go in New Orleans in July, and I knew I'd never return to the office or the taproom, that I would pack my bag and leave the widow's house in the middle of the night and not go back, and while the kiss went on and on and on, I swore to myself Mrs. Erickson was the last woman I would ever touch, and until I met Nadine, I kept that vow.

Eighteen years in Munich, sixteen in New Orleans, childhood and adulthood, the former loud and crowded, the latter quiet and spacious. After I broke from Mrs. Erickson's kiss, I found the hardest part of being alone was not my desire to touch or talk to or kiss others—I had no such desire—but others' desire to touch or talk to or kiss me. People are for the most part kindhearted, and most equate solitude with loneliness.

The first years of my solitary life I spent a lot of time running away from the well-intentioned. I was young, I wasn't ugly, and in barrooms men attempted to josh with me about Ruth and Gehrig and DiMaggio. In movie house lobbies girls tried to chat me up about the weather. On the streetcar old ladies asked after my wife— fiancée? girlfriend? I found it was easy to get people to leave me alone. I put on flab (blue plates, milkshakes), wore a shirt that was too small, grew fuzzy muttonchops. When someone came in my direction, I grinned widely, rubbed my hands together, and licked my teeth.

I walked the parks alone, rode all the streetcar routes noting the libraries and the newsstands and the movie theaters they could take me to. In summer I went out to Pontchartrain Beach, rolled up my cuffs, and waded in the lake; in February I watched Mardi Gras parades by myself. One day I absentmindedly picked up the *Item*, and immediately I began to need the morning and afternoon newspapers as badly as I needed the cups of coffee I drank while reading them. I joined the legion of men who live in workingmen's hotels and sit alone at lunch counters studying box scores while eating their dinners.

After Mr. Erickson skipped town with his tart, I got a job frying doughnuts at a bakery run by an ancient New Orleanian with an affected French accent that disappeared when he grew angry. At the bakery I spoke only when spoken to and kept my answers short. I once overheard someone describe me as "the shy fellow." I worked my way up to night baker, the perfect job for somebody who wants to be alone.

I followed a season of baseball by way of the "Baseball Barometer" and impatiently waited through the winter for another season to begin. In the spring of '29 I went to watch a game I saw advertised in the paper, the Pelicans versus the Tulane College boys. Someone in the bleachers assured me the teams were the city's best, but the keen disappointment I felt seeing the players clumsily enact the game I'd seen only in my imagination made me vow never to watch another. I subscribed to the *Sporting News*, translated numbers and names into lovely games.

My dark hours were filled with cakes and pastries, and when I couldn't sleep, there was plenty to do if I got dressed and walked the streets at noontime, my bright midnight. The bakery survived the stock market's crash and the lean times that followed, but when Old Man Hebert died, his twin grandsons sold the ovens and fired us all. That was '38, the year I started at Hubig's. My experience and a good recommendation from the twins who'd never met me meant not much changed in my life.

I stayed away from all things German, even food, the thing I missed most. I heard the language spoken in the street now and again, and for many years when I did, I expected to turn and find my cousin, but the more I ignored anything not American, the more every language that was not English faded into babble. When Hitler invaded Poland, my decade of avoiding German social clubs and newspapers and ignoring insults muttered in Munich slang seemed brilliant foresight, not a simpleminded attempt to fight off the many symptoms of homesickness.

I read the widow's obituary in November of 1939, and that same day in a department store on Canal Street I came face to face with Harold, the bartender from the taproom on South Solomon. At first I was relieved he didn't recognize me, but as he walked to the elevator, I was stricken with sadness when I thought of how few people in the city in which I'd lived for more than a decade knew my face, let alone my name. I had a boy shine my shoes just so I could introduce myself. He was embarrassed not to know who I was. I shaved my sideburns as soon as I got back to my room.

After Sammy uncorked the bottle I'd been living in, I thought a lot about the time I'd spent alone. How had I filled the days, months, years? Baseball, movies, mysteries, the warm brown smells of the bakery—and what else? I'd be lying if I claimed I wasn't lonely then. Many days I wanted so badly to speak to someone that I buried my face in my pillow and talked myself to sleep the way my widowed mother had once cried herself. Sixteen years of solitude left me nearly unable to remember why I wanted to be alone in the first place.

◆◆◆

We met at Katz's soda fountain on Canal Street. I'd seen them before, at the Orpheum, the Mecca, the Garden, the little Laurel where you had to check the paper to be sure there would be a movie and not a talent show or vaudeville. We three fatsoes hid in the dark watching newsreels and cartoons, musicals and love stories, Lauren Bacall and Tarzan and Abbott and Costello. I didn't know their names, but over months of Saturdays and Sundays I'd passed him coming and going from men's rooms, and I'd stood behind her in line to buy popcorn and candy. We always looked away, pretended we couldn't see each other even though we were too big for anyone to ignore. He climbed to the balcony, she hurried down to the front row, and I sat in the back with the snoring ushers. She hid her thick arms in a pink sweater, no matter the season. He never wore a hat, and his hair was thick and dark and carefully combed. Once I accidentally looked into her face and was surprised by the feline yellow of her eyes.

That day in Katz's he and I sat at either end of the counter, she in a booth, as far away from one another as we could, ashamed by the space we filled and the food we ordered. I watched him examine his reflection in the polished surface of a napkin dispenser, then stand and cross the room and ask if he could join her. She looked terrified, but nodded. I was amazed and jealous, as well as embarrassed for them—two fatties eating hot fudge sundaes, a joke for the gum-popping schoolgirls and the soda jerk to share—then surprised by the joy I felt when he turned and waved me over. I gathered my meal and struggled into the booth beside him.

"What's the good word, slim? This is Nadine," he said.

I took the cool hand she offered and gave her my name, she told me his, and suddenly we three were best friends. Sammy was animated, laughing, doing imitations from movies. The distance we'd kept disappeared.

The diet was Sammy's idea. "No more ice cream, no more Cokes, no more potatoes," he told us one day while we stood in line to buy tickets at the National. Only three weeks had passed since he'd brought us together in Katz's.

"Potatoes?" Nadine said. "What's wrong with potatoes?"

He poked her soft belly with two fingers, and I thought she was going to cry.

"What about fried chicken?" I asked to save her feelings.

He shook his head sadly. "Walter, are you joking? Fried chicken?"

Nadine blew her nose and blinked back tears.

"Same with fried shrimp, I guess," I said. "And fried oysters."

Sammy nodded slowly, as if humoring a halfwit.

The nodding was more than I could stand. "You're fat too," I reminded him, and Nadine hid her smile behind her handkerchief.

We watched the movie with our hands in our laps, no double-buttered popcorn or rattling boxes of Raisinets. I cannot remember what we saw; all I recall is hunger. Afterward, when we went to Walgreen's, Sammy ordered three coffees and three health salads. The waitress knew us and thought he was kidding. She waited with her pencil ready over her pad for our serious orders. "Please," Nadine begged her. The salads were cold piles of cottage cheese topped with canned fruit cocktail, each plate decorated with a single limp lettuce leaf. I was so hungry I could read Nadine's mind—*banana split, hamburger, chocolate malted.* Sammy forked a pear slice into his mouth and grinned. We drank our coffee black.

There was no reason for us not to cheat, no way we'd get caught breaking Sammy's rules. He worked for Brown's Dairy and could've gorged on gallons of ice cream; I could've eaten dozens of Hubig's fried pies. Nadine looked after a gaggle of children for a neighbor and could've baked cakes for the kids and taken more than her share. The rationing helped our diets. There was simply less butter, less sugar, less meat, fewer eggs, and being fat was not patriotic.

On weekends Sammy led us on forced marches through City Park, cheered when the number on the pharmacy's scale was smaller than it had been the Sunday before, wrote lists of foods we should avoid, increased the numbers of jumping jacks and knee bends we were to do first thing every morning. We sneaked bananas into the movies in Nadine's purse and sipped ice water afterward. When one day I bought a forbidden Coca-Cola, I could take only a single sweet sip before guilt made me pour it into the gutter.

Sammy was a know-it-all and a blowhard. Whatever the subject, he was an expert, and it made me jealous to see Nadine hang on every word of his boorish and usually inaccurate lectures on the history of traffic lights or the Chinese origins of hard candy. She laughed at his stupid jokes, even when she was the butt of them. I didn't correct him when I knew the truth, didn't defend her when he made fun. As much as he annoyed me, he also delighted me, and I wasn't surprised Nadine was delighted as well. The longer I knew her the clearer it became she'd been hurt badly, perhaps by someone just like Sammy, and what seemed to me incessant lessons and mean cracks might be to her the kind of attention dumb men think all women want. I began to think of Nadine as Sammy's girl, and I hoped the day I was no longer welcome to tag along with them was slow in coming.

We shrank, slowly at first, then faster. The third month I went down two holes on my belt, the next I had to punch more holes, then I had to buy a new belt. Nadine took in our pants over and over. We shrank through the summer months and into October, fall's cool and our better health coming at the same time so I was never sure which was truly to thank for making me sweat less. Sammy's red face lightened; Nadine's yellow eyes seemed to grow larger. All of us began to look our true ages, Nadine younger than she had appeared, Sammy and I older.

The numbers in Sammy's notebook grew smaller. By Halloween he'd shed 49 pounds, Nadine had lost 37, and I'd dropped from 243 to 180. I couldn't believe the scale—*63 pounds?*—but the next morning I looked in the mirror and noticed the smooth dent on the side of each of my buttocks, something I hadn't seen since I'd arrived in New Orleans. Stretch marks crisscrossed my shrunken body. I looked like I'd been smashed and my pieces glued back together.

The world seemed bigger around me. I felt as if I'd moved to a city built on a larger scale—seats in the movies and on the streetcar, lavatory doors, soda fountain stools. I began to hate fat people, and my hatred grew almost in proportion to the pounds I lost. There was something morally wrong in choosing to be portly when you could be svelte. The fat were weak, greedy, unpatriotic. There was something dirty about them too, a belief proven correct when one night a wen that had been on my back for years opened after I had been doing jumping jacks. A pearl of pus appeared, and when I pinched the lump, more pus came out. I kept squeezing, gagging at what I saw in the bathroom mirror. In the end I expressed more than a tablespoon of the stinking opalescent mess that had been sealed under the layer of flab my toe touches and knee bends had stripped away.

On a November Saturday six months after we met, we walked the three miles downtown to Canal—"Every step counts," Sammy reminded us—so we men could buy new suits and Nadine could find a frock and a pair of pumps. In Krauss we did a poor job hiding our amazement at inches subtracted, sizes halved. Sammy bought seersucker, I chose blue serge, and Nadine picked a dress the color of her eyes. We were new people in our new duds. We left our fat clothes behind in the dressing rooms.

It was bright and breezy as springtime, and we went to the French Market and ordered our coffee black out of habit, not because we were lardy slobs who dreamed of being thin. We took the St. Charles streetcar Uptown, a treat sweet as Coke or Hershey's. Sammy got off at Jackson to walk to his Irish Channel apartment, and we laughed as he hugged and then kissed a lamppost, something a funny drunk had done in a movie we'd seen the week before. A few blocks along Nadine pulled the cord, and when I leaned to give her cheek the usual chaste good-bye kiss, she took my hand and pulled me to my feet and led me off the car.

She lived just off the Avenue on Conery Street, in what must've once been a maid's quarters, behind a Garden District mansion that had become a rooming house. From Nadine's miniature front porch I could see the north gates of Lafayette Cemetery #1 and the ghostly crypts behind the iron bars. I'd been inside the maisonette only once before, a week or two after Sammy had introduced us all, when we came to surprise her on her birthday and found Nadine alone, finishing an entire cake. The little house was a rectangle divided into two squares, flimsy door between, one square bedroom and parlor, the other kitchen and bath, a curtain half-hiding toilet and tub from stove and sink.

She pulled her mail from the box and showed me a picture postcard of palm trees. "My sister, in Florida." Once we were inside, Nadine looked like she'd forgotten why I was there. I was afraid to move. We stood in opposite corners of the tiny parlor and looked at each other's feet. The streetcar clicked over a crossing on St. Charles, and I wondered if it was annoying or soothing to hear that all day and night.

Nadine's eyes were the color of honey. "That's a really nice dress," I told her.

She turned to a mirror and went on tiptoe. "Take it off me," she whispered to her reflection. She lifted her hair so I could work the zipper. I pinched the pull and slid it halfway down. When I stopped, she said, "Keep going." She stepped out of her dress and said again, "Keep going." I unsnapped her brassiere and rolled down her stockings. Nadine was pale and lovely, naked save a pair of panties the pink of her nipples. She said, "Keep going," and I hooked my trembling thumbs into the waistband of her underwear and pulled it down. She choked me when she tried to loosen my new tie, so I hurriedly undressed myself while she turned down the quilt.

When I pushed into her, she said "Ouch," but when I stopped and asked, "Ouch?" she said, "Keep going." She kissed my neck and wrapped one of her legs around one of mine and sighed when I put my hand under her smooth behind, and when I lifted myself and climaxed onto her hip, she reached up and put her hand to my chest to feel my heart hammering my ribs.

She called me "Bobby" from the bathtub. "Who's Bobby?" I asked, and she opened the tap. Over the splashing water and humming pipes I thought I heard her crying. I stopped tying my shoes and went to the door. "Are you all right?" I pressed my ear to the paint and heard only water. We'd kissed and wrestled in her narrow bed until the afternoon faded and the room lost its colors, but I wasn't sure it was appropriate for me to see her in her bath. The tap closed.

"Nadine?" I knocked *shave and a haircut.* "You all right?" I heard what sounded like water on the floor, feared the tub was overflowing, that she was drowning herself, and I twisted the knob. She was standing in front of the stove, naked and dripping bathwater, measuring grounds into a percolator. I'd forgotten that the kitchen shared space with the bath, and for a moment I was disoriented.

"Coffee?" she asked the pot, her voice wobbling.

"Yes, please," I said. I found a towel and dried her off, fetched for her a flannel nightgown from the dresser.

Bobby was her dead husband, killed in the Pacific in '42, and his death was the reason she'd gotten fat. "Hard to cry when your mouth's full of potatoes and fried chicken," she explained.

I nodded, taking her seriously, and she laughed at me and touched a fingertip to my eyebrow. "Lucky boy. I wish I was just hungry like you." We sat side by side on the bed, not speaking, her head on my shoulder. Out the window, black silhouettes in the shapes of trees were pasted onto the gray-blue sky. It felt like Nadine was hiccuping when she began again to cry. I licked tears off her chin, and she didn't flinch. Her eyes were so lovely—honey, caramel, toffee—that I expected sugar on my tongue, not salt.

After years of penny-pinching, I had more than six thousand dollars in the bank. I remembered Eckart's cashbox each time I totaled the numbers in my bankbook, but the war erased what little guilt time had not.

The day we were to be married, Nadine and I took a cab to Adler's Jewelry on Canal, where, to my chagrin, she picked the simplest ring she could find. She still had the strand of yellow wire with a chip of flawed something Bobby had given her, and while she didn't wear it, knowing she kept it pressed like a flower in her Bible convinced me grand gestures were in order. I suggested a diamond the size of an ice cube, but she shook her head and checked the fit of a plain gold band.

She was wearing the yellow dress she'd bought the day she led me off the streetcar, the day I asked her to marry me, and I was wearing the same blue serge suit. I watched her decide between two rings and remembered unzipping the yellow dress and grew excited knowing soon I would be unzipping it again.

I told the cabbie what errand we were running, and he waited outside the jeweler's though I asked him not to, meter off, a wedding gift. He was an old Italian who made jokes about sex while he drove us to the courthouse. "There will be no sleeping on this night! The tired wife is the happy wife! The marriage bed is bent in the frame!"

Nadine was blushing, looking out the window at nothing. I tried to tip him when we made it to Tulane Avenue, but he waved off the money and winked at Nadine. When he drove away, his gift complete, we both burst into nervous laughter. I held out my hand.

Sammy was waiting inside, our witness. He too wore the suit he'd bought that day on Canal. A friend of his hadn't arrived to be our second witness, but Sammy had found a plump woman named Emma, whom, he explained, he had met before, at another courthouse wedding.

"I don't work here," she confided. "I just love seeing people getting married, so I come down every day. This will be my ninety-third this year." She pulled a comb from her purse and led Nadine into a corner to fix her hair.

The Justice of the Peace greeted Emma by name, complimented her hat, and had Nadine and me repeat fewer vows than I'd expected. Emma wept, blew her nose, signed her name below Sammy's, then spotted another couple across the hall and wished us health and many children.

Nadine and I stood holding hands at the top of the courthouse steps, blinking and squinting in the pure afternoon light of December in Louisiana. She was on my right, and I could feel her ring against my fingers. Trucks passed on Tulane Avenue, a streetcar's bells rang—I wanted to remember everything. The air smelled of exhaust and cut grass, fried fish and the river.

Sammy took us to Antoine's, told all the waiters we were newlyweds, ordered champagne. After oysters Rockefeller and another bottle of champagne, Nadine slipped her foot from her shoe and rubbed my ankle with her toe while I tickled the inside of her knee. She chirped when I eased my hand up between her thighs.

Sammy shook his head and grinned. He ordered *Gateau chocolat d'Yvonne,* and Nadine stared at her piece of chocolate cake for a long time before she picked up her fork, bent forward, and started eating. Tears filled her eyes, and when she finished, I slid my plate in front of her. She cut a huge bite and filled her mouth with it. I knew it had to be Bobby she was thinking of while she ate and cried. Sammy watched her, then looked at me and raised his eyebrows. He offered her his piece, but she declined, blew her nose into her napkin, wiped her lips, and grabbed me by the ears and kissed me hard. Bobby was gone, but I was sitting beside her.

At the curb Sammy passed me a key on a heavy fob. "Monteleone," he said. "Neither of you has a place nice enough for a wedding night."

Nadine hugged him and joked, "What's the good word?"

"How can you afford all this?" I asked.

He shrugged. "My horse won."

In the hotel elevator I picked her up and we kissed as the floors dinged past, the porter politely staring at the numbers. I carried her over the threshold, tipped the boy who'd led us to the door, slammed it behind him, dropped Nadine on the bed, unzipped the yellow dress, and kissed the spools of her spine. When I rose to put out the light, she pulled me down. "Walt, I want to see you, Walt."

She said my name while I kissed her breasts, when I pushed inside her, when she arched her back, when afterward we tickled each other and wrestled and then surprised ourselves with another time in the wide, soft bed.

I woke first, my face tight and my skull stuffed with the cotton wool of a champagne hangover. I opened the curtains and raised the sash to drink cold air and listen to the Quarter—tugboat horns, a mule's clattering, someone whistling a Tommy Dorsey song. I turned down the sheet and admired my wife—*my wife*, I thought, the words clearing my head. Her hair was fanned across the pillow in a golden crown; her neck was rosy from the stubble on my cheeks; her nipples were pink and perfect; her bellybutton begged for my tongue, the tangle below it a shade darker than the hair on her head, the mystery of blondes.

She woke and smiled and rolled her eyes when she saw my erection.

◆◆◆

Nadine picked our house, convinced me it was best to live Uptown, though it meant a long streetcar ride to and from work. I switched to the day shift and learned again how to sleep through the night, this time with Nadine beside me. She'd been working a few days a week at the notions counter at Holmes and babysitting to make ends meet, but I told her she should quit both, and she did.

The house at 728 Milan had a sound roof, a fresh coat of paint inside, and a new stove. It was a shotgun, each room leading to the next—first parlor, second, big bedroom, little bedroom, bathroom, kitchen—a kind of house I'd never seen before I came to New Orleans. I emptied my bank account and paid cash for the place two days after Christmas. I tied a bow to the key, and Nadine cried for joy when I gave it to her. My frugal, lonely years meant I had enough to afford a new Frigidaire icebox, a stove, and a mattress and bed frame.

The day in early January when we moved in, a neighbor from up the block brought me a bottle of beer, introduced himself as Clem, and told me who my other neighbors were. Bobby's sister lived to my right in 726 Milan, his grandfather to my left in 730. Another sister was directly across the street in 729, and his mother was next to her in 727. In 727's window the widow's flag with its gold star was for her husband; the mother's with its blue was for Bobby.

"Lost both her men to the Japs." Clem shook his head and drained his beer.

He told me the sisters were married and each had two kids, a total of three boys and a girl. Four generations of Zancas surrounded me. I heard Nadine inside, unpacking boxes and happily humming. She wore a locket with Bobby's grinning face inside—I'd opened it one night while she slept and known at once who he was—but I'd explained this as the pain of losing her first love, told myself I was foolish to be jealous of the dead.

Clem knocked his empty Jax bottle on the porch floor and stood to leave. "Look on your face tells me this is news to you."

I didn't say anything. Across the street a cat lay in a puddle of sunlight. I could sell the house and buy another somewhere Bobby's people did not live: by City Park; further Uptown, on the other side of the zoo. I felt like a sucker. I wondered if she would've married anyone she knew had the money to afford the house. Then I remembered how shocked she'd been when I showed her my bankbook the day we went to buy our rings. She'd accepted my proposal when she thought I was poor. But once she found out about the money and picked the house, didn't she think I'd figure out I was encircled by her dead husband's relatives? And didn't she think that would upset me?

She was unwrapping newspaper from around salt and pepper shakers when I went inside.

"Why do you want to live here?" I asked.

She looked up from a pair of peacocks. "It's a lovely house."

"What about the Zancas?"

Her smile fluttered. "Bobby's dead, Walt," she said without hesitation. "I'm married to you. I picked this house because I like it, and because I know these people—I don't know many people—and it makes sense to me to settle down around people I know, people who know me. Does that make sense?"

I thought about my many years of loneliness, nearly half my life spent alone, and agreed that it made sense.

That night Nadine cried when she smelled Bobby's cigarette— his grandfather, Dom, smoking an after-dinner Lucky on his back stoop. The next day she burst into tears when Bobby's mother, Sylvia, turned away and pretended not to hear when Nadine called a greeting. None of the Zancas would talk to her.

January passed, then Lent, and Bobby haunted our house. His spirit manifested itself in Nadine's wish that his mother would speak to her, his sisters invite her into their kitchens to gossip, their children call her Auntie. Some days I wondered if I was anything more than a stand-in for Bobby. But then Nadine would turn and catch me looking at her while she darned a sock or mixed cake batter, and she'd smile at me in a way that made it clear she wasn't smiling at a ghost, she was smiling at me.

We lived with Bobby Zanca all around us, his people yelling at each other and smoking his cigarettes and boiling his coffee, the cat that was a kitten when he named it Rascal marking its territory so that each time it rained the acrid smell of tomcat urine came up through the floorboards.

One day through the kitchen window I spied one of Bobby's sisters whispering to Nadine over the fence that divided her backyard from ours. When she came inside, Nadine sat down at the table and sighed. "His mother thinks I'm a whore for marrying you instead of wearing a black dress for the rest of my life," she said. "None of them are allowed to speak to me."

"We can move."

She shook her head and took a long breath, then shrugged. "They're just the neighbors," she said.

Inside 728 the Schmidts read the newspaper, tumbled in bed, ate at the little kitchen table, turned the radio up too loudly—who cared what the neighbors thought? Sammy came to dinner on Sundays. When he and I sat on the back stoop drinking beer and listening to Nadine wash dishes, he told me how lucky I was to have her.

"You owe me for this," he reminded me every week.

◆◆◆

Everyone who worked at Hubig's helped by breaking the rationing rules and giving the bakery what they could: a pound of sugar, a dozen eggs, a tire so the trucks could deliver. It was better to drink your morning coffee black—or skip it—than to go without a job. Still, some days we quit at noon because there was nothing for us to bake, and Monday was one of those days. After we spent the morning shift frying apple pies, the foreman announced there were no eggs for the afternoon's scheduled run of lemon and sent us home.

I took the Gentilly car to Lee Circle and transferred to the St. Charles. The sun had burned away the morning haze, and I hoped I could persuade Nadine to pack a picnic lunch we could take to the park. My mouth watered at the thought of cold chicken, the precious can of peaches I knew she'd been saving, a bottle of beer. Lost in picnic daydreams, I missed my stop. I got off the streetcar at Napoleon, headed back the two blocks to Milan, and turned toward the river.

The neighborhood cats were rolling in puddles of sunlight, the kids at McDonogh Number 7 were screaming and playing tag, and behind shutters, housewives like Nadine were listening to cheery music coming from their radios while they ironed their husbands' shirts. I greeted the postman, waved to the old folks sitting on their porches, asked and was asked, "Pretty day?"

I'd been walking this route to and from the streetcar stop for nearly four months, and slowly but surely I'd started to think of the narrow houses with their beds of cheery flowers, and the stolid school, and even the cats as *mine*. I felt bad for being greedy, covetous, but then I decided the proprietary urges I felt were no more than neighborliness. Perhaps this was Americanness, rooted in me at last.

The gardenia in my front yard was blooming, and it smelled as if someone had broken a jug of perfume on the steps. I picked a big blossom and turned the knob carefully, hoping to surprise Nadine.

The bedroom door was open, and she and Sammy were tangled together. My heart tore when I saw them, but I didn't make a sound. Nadine was on her back, and Sammy moved over her. She had her knees bent and her heels dug into the mattress, and the curve of her tensed hip mirrored the curve of his. I didn't mean to tiptoe through the front rooms, but while my heart was ripping, I couldn't ignore how beautiful Nadine and Sammy had become, and I wondered if I too was that lovely when she held me. This is why I didn't yell, why it didn't occur to me to hunt for a hatchet or a pistol to kill my best friend and my wife.

Sammy yelped when he finally saw me, but vanity took my voice while he rolled off Nadine and the bed and slammed to the floor. Beauty froze my rage even though Nadine made no attempt to cover herself. I knew I was supposed to slap her, but in the dim bedroom, her skin was flawless.

Sammy got up, and I looked away from his wilting penis, foreskin creased and jaundiced, looked back, saw it was a rubber, not foreskin, and looked away again. His keys and coins chimed in his pockets as he danced into his trousers.

"What's the good word, Walter?" he asked, his usual greeting sounding like an obscenity, then added, "Sorry."

"Sammy," I said, then said again, "Sammy."

"Don't talk to him," Nadine snapped, and though she was looking at me, it was not clear which of us she was shushing.

Sammy looked at her, then at me, then back at her.

Nadine rose from the bed and stood unashamed in the doorway, her feet apart and her hands on her hips, a pose that suggested calisthenics more than it did adultery. I closed my eyes when I couldn't look away from the brassy tangle between her legs. Next to me was the lamp I'd bought her, beside it the curio cabinet filled with her collection of animal-shaped salt and pepper shakers. We movables stood on the Turkey rug for which I'd paid a week's wages because Nadine liked its pattern and colors. I'd read enough dime novels and seen enough B movies to know I was supposed to shout *I give you all these things, and this is how you repay me?* Nadine plucked the gardenia from my fist and tucked it behind her ear. Her hand shook.

Sammy held a shoe in each hand. "Walter," he apologized, and bolted past me.

The front door banged closed behind him, and in the quiet that followed I heard the kitchen tap drip at the opposite end of the house. I examined the rug's pattern so I wouldn't have to look at Nadine.

"What kind of man walks in on *that* and doesn't do anything or even *say* anything?"

"You're mad at me?" I was expecting a stammered apology, a clumsy explanation. "Unbelievable."

"*Own-bee-lieb-ah-bowl*," she mocked in a thick German accent I do not have.

I pushed past her into the bedroom. It stank of sweat and hair tonic.

"I paid for this house," I reminded her. "I paid *cash*."

Nadine took the gardenia from behind her ear and slowly tore off its petals. "You stupid Kraut." She sniffed and blinked back tears. "What kind of man opens the door and sees his wife fucking his best friend and doesn't even *yell*?"

I slapped her, and she folded to the floor, and in her wide eyes I was startled to see relief.

I put my hat on top of the wardrobe, hung my jacket, unbuttoned my shirt, the things I did every day when I came home from work. I hoped routine would look like rage, hoped I'd appear to be so angry that all I could manage to do was to take off my shirt when in truth all I could think to do was to take off my shirt. It was the first time I'd ever heard her say *fucking*.

I stuffed my hands into my pockets to stop myself from helping her up. "Take a bath and put some clothes on," I ordered. "Cook my dinner."

Nadine pulled the sheet off the bed to cover herself. I walked the short hall between bedroom and kitchen, everything ugly catching my eye—forks and spoons and knives sunk in hazy dishwater, cracked windowpane above the sink, my filthy fingerprints around the back door's knob. On the other side of my little backyard's head-high fence, a radio muttered what was surely more bad news. The potted lemon tree I watered and worried over was blooming, each flower smelling like a distillation of the fruit it would become. I stood sniffing the blossoms below a sky so blue it looked enameled.

The beauty I'd seen when I'd walked in on them faded completely when it occurred to me that this is what I'd once feared would happen—Nadine would pick Sammy, not me—and I felt foolish for getting over that fear, and then I felt pain, and though it was sharp and deep, I knew it was only a pale version of the pain Andreas had felt when he sent Ilse off to kill the baby I'd claimed might be mine, not even a tickle compared to the pain he'd felt when she died obeying his command.

I'd left behind in Munich all manner of sadness, and in New Orleans I'd found happiness, my sins unknown to my neighbors and eventually nearly forgotten by me. What kind of man was I? Walking home from the streetcar I thought I was a happy American without a care in the world, but I couldn't yell when I caught my wife in bed with my best friend. My lemon tree smelled foreign, my sky looked odd, my melancholy felt German.

Nadine and I did not speak at the dinner table, and after I ate I left without telling her where I was going. I rode the Magazine car down to Jackson, walked two blocks toward the river, and found Sammy sitting on his steps. "What's the good word?" he hailed as if nothing had happened. I had to bend down to hit him. He touched the trickle of blood that came from the corner of his mouth, examined the finger, and then, without standing, hit me in my stomach.

I doubled over, and he stood and patiently waited for me to straighten, and accepted my punch to his breadbasket without lifting his hands. He wheezed and gasped while I shook the pain out of my fingers. When he caught his breath, he hit my ear. It was still ringing when I socked him in the nose. He staggered and blinked over and over. Run out of his own ideas, he punched my nose. It was clear neither of us was going to defend himself. We hit each other's jaws, and I spat my upper plate into my hand while he tongued loose teeth. When I kicked him in the testicles, Sammy turned his head and puked a red and viscous mess.

"My God, is that *pie*?"

"Shut up," he gagged, and for the first time the fight seemed dangerous.

I jammed my teeth back into my mouth. "Fuck you," I told him, and punched him in the stomach to see what else was in there. He hit back with a quick combination—right to the cheek, left to the neck—and I knew the rules had changed. I squared up and raised my fists, ready to kill him, finally, for what he'd done.

"Woman!" an old voice yelled before I could throw my punches. Sammy and I turned. Across Annunciation an elderly neighbor stood in an open door. "Woman!" the octogenarian bellowed again.

"Yes," Sammy admitted, and I realized the old man had guessed why we were fighting.

He looked pleased with himself. "Stop it, jackasses," he commanded, and slammed shut his door.

We stood gaping at nothing, both of us breathing hard. A car passed, a little dog barking in its window.

"That was Mister Henry," Sammy said. "The old man, not the dog."

He made a pot of tea, and we sat at his kitchen table sipping it and painting our cut knuckles with mercurochrome. Sammy put the last piece of cherry pie on a plate. "I loved her when she was ugly," he said when he served it to me.

I pushed his pie away. My nose began to bleed again when I blew into my handkerchief. "She picked me." I was too angry to say anything else.

"I loved her when she was ugly," he tried again.

"She was never ugly." I wanted to remember the moment I opened the door and saw them, the way their beauty had stunned me more than any of his punches, but because of his insistence that when fat, Nadine had been ugly, and he alone had loved fat Nadine, all I could remember was fat Sammy and fat Nadine—and fat me— and I wondered if he was telling the truth that his love was more forgiving, mine less.

"Never talk to her again."

"What?" He looked like I'd told him I murdered her after he left.

"Never. Talk. To her. Again."

"But Walt," he whined, "she's my friend."

"Not anymore."

"But Walter, Walty, Walt-o, you two are my *best* friends."

"Next you'll tell me you loved me when I was ugly."

He looked heartbroken. "You're my only friends."

I went to the sink and rinsed my handkerchief. "You should've thought about friendship before you did what you did."

His split bottom lip was wobbling when I turned to him. Sammy opened his mouth but couldn't find words. From the bedroom he fetched a shoebox. There was no telling what was inside—gun, Bible, can of cherry pie filling—and I didn't lean to see when he took off the lid.

"Please," he begged, and I looked. The box was full of money.

The sight of the carefully stacked and rubberbanded greenbacks dazed me.

"Thousand dollars," he said. "Take it."

It was another insult, not an apology, and I wondered if he was actually so stupid he didn't know. If there'd been a gun in the box with the money, I would've picked it up and shot him. If there had been a knife, I would've cut his throat.

"Where did you get this?" I asked.

His face twisted as if I'd offended him. "None of your business."

"She's not a whore."

"I never said she was." His tone remained snotty.

"You're offering me a thousand dollars after I catch you in bed with my wife, and you think that's not calling her a whore?"

"Look," he said, "take it or don't take it."

What kind of man did it make me when I slapped on the lid and tucked the box under my arm?

I walked home thinking of my childhood, a time I'd not allowed myself to remember for many years. When we were little boys in Munich, my cousin and I played a game where we locked arms and sprinted backwards along an icy street until one of us lost his footing. The winner fell on top of the loser as hard as he could. When we got too good at staying on our feet, we had to figure out new ways to trip each other, and so we began to knock other people down. One of the game's few rules was that we couldn't look over our shoulders to see what or who was behind us, so we had to trust our ears. Old ladies muttering were easy to hear, and they screamed even if only bumped. The policemen were too old or infirm or cowardly to go away to war like our fathers, and they became our favorite targets—we listened for their womanish gossiping. One day Andreas bounced me off the ragpicker's mule and I cut my face on its harness, but I managed somehow to keep my balance and to slam him into the tinsmith's cart. The noise was like the sound of the end of the world: braying mule, pots and pans clattering on cobblestones. We fell down, still arm in arm, while the tinsmith yelled for a policeman whom we'd surely knocked down at some point. A ladle's handle slashed Andreas just below his eye. I remember knowing immediately that when one of our mothers painted our cuts with iodine and we looked into the mirror, our wounds would match.

In New Orleans I crossed Austerlitz backwards, ready to hear a horn, ready to be run over by a truck. I watched the way I'd come until I tripped over the curb on the opposite side of the street and fell heavily onto my ass.

I dreamt that horns sprouted from my temples. First they were a kid's nubs, but quickly they grew to a billy's points and kept growing. My antlers curled like a cartoon Lucifer's and then corkscrewed like something you'd see in the *National Geographic Magazine.* Even while I was asleep it was an easy dream to understand, but I woke on the couch in the middle of the night holding my head and groaning. I'd been too upset to get into bed with Nadine, though what I wanted to do when I got back from Sammy's was to take his place in the scene into which I'd earlier stumbled.

I was cold when I woke from my nightmare and found myself alone on the sofa. The thin blanket wasn't enough to stop my shivering—I was used to Nadine's heat beside me. I dressed in the clothes I'd worn the day before and lay down again. There was no trace of dawn in the transom above the front door. I wondered why Nadine had done it and then felt like an idiot for not wondering before. I wanted to believe it would've been naive of me to suppose there was a single reason, but maybe the truth was simple: I wasn't Bobby; I was the reason the Zancas shunned her. I hoped her motives were more complex.

She hadn't wanted me to catch her—I came home hours before she expected me—so her intent wasn't to hurt me or to make me hurt her or Sammy. Her anger over my reaction wasn't because she had planned to see me act in a way I didn't. It was a mistake, not a test. I thought of Bobby's face in her locket, of Sammy saying he'd loved her when she was ugly, and it pained me that Nadine could ignore the truth that I loved her more than any ghost or blow-hard ever could, that I had loved her the moment I met her, not just when she was thin. Jealousy, envy, and spite were why Sammy had done it. I knew it because I suffered from those maladies in Munich—they led me to lie to my cousin—and in New Orleans I suffered them when I'd once thought Nadine liked Sammy, not me, and I suffered them again as soon as I recovered from the shock of seeing my wife and my friend together. Maybe I was right when I guessed someone like Sammy had hurt her—maybe it'd been Bobby—and maybe she thought being hurt like that again would make the first hurt fade, or bring it back. Lying on the couch, I felt like a child again, embarrassed by my stupidity, a puzzle filling my brain with noise until sleep silenced things.

My head was still hurting from dreams and the punches Sammy had given it when I woke to birdcalls and the smacks of newspapers on porches. I went outside and pissed into the gardenia bush, hoping a Zanca or two was watching from behind her shutters. I drank from the hose and then held it over my head. I combed my wet hair with my fingers and listened to church bells ring six. The last was still echoing when the cranes began to fly over, a dozen at a time, hundreds of them heading downriver, low over the housetops, perfectly silent. In one squadron a blue heron was made black by the bleached birds around it. It felt like an omen I should understand. Was I the dark bird?

I stole Dom Zanca's newspaper and snapped its rubber band at Rascal.

On the front page was a map with arrows representing the Allied offensive poking deep into Germany from several angles. Plans to close the bars for V-E Day had been in place for a month, I read.

Below the fold was news that the river was rising dangerously. Upriver in Ponte-a-la-Hache, Port Sulfur, and Reserve, German POWs were fighting the flooding with sandbags and wash fences. I knew about the POWs—they were in New Orleans too—but knowing there were German prisoners in the city was important only because we were at war and they were our enemies. I'd seen them filling potholes and weeding flowerbeds in Audubon Park, pale men and boys in convicts' stripes with POW lettered across their backs. Sammy told me they'd surrendered in North Africa, and at the time my only thought was how odd it was to witness German soldiers who'd been captured in Africa pulling weeds in a New Orleans park. I hadn't looked closely, and the second time I saw them I'd assumed I was seeing the same dozen, but when I read the list of towns where the POWs were up on the levees—Tallulah, Slocum, Marksville, Simmesport, Innis—I wondered how many *Häftlinge* were in Louisiana. Not enough to fight off the river, according to the paper. Citizens were asked to come and help. I wished I could, wished for a way to prove to myself and everyone else that I loved my second country and hated my first—even if bits of the language of the first that I thought I'd purged from my memory were beginning to invade my thoughts.

There was news of a man accused of spying for the Germans in Baton Rouge. Early in the war an immigrant named Schmidt had been caught in New Orleans sending shortwave messages about troop movements. I'd been baffled by my namesake's treason, but now I wondered how different he was from me. What kind of man was I? I thought I knew the answer: good husband, good American, good friend. But if I was the kind of man who stood silently ogling my wife and best friend in bed, and the kind who accepted a shoebox full of money as recompense for what I'd seen, maybe I was the kind who would hide in an attic to whisper into a transmitter about how many men boarded ships.

The casualty lists filled a page. The dead got their pictures in the *Picayune*, and I thought of Bobby when I looked at grinning Arthur Landry and somber Roland Waguespack. She still loved him enough to want to be near his family, enough to suffer their cruelty just to hear their voices. I wanted her to love me that much. Maybe that's why I didn't yell—I was the kind of man who'd do anything to make her love me.

I went inside and shook Nadine awake. "I'm the kind of man who will do anything to make you love me," I told her.

She looked bewildered. "It was only that once, I want you to know."

I felt like a fool for not considering there might've been other times. "I should have killed him," I said. I wanted to tell her that her beauty had kept me from even thinking of killing at the time, but it didn't seem like something the kind of man I wanted her to know I was would admit to. "I went to his house and beat him up," I bragged. "That's where I got these cuts and bruises." I showed her my skinned knuckles.

Nadine nodded, and I fought the urge to ask why she'd done it: She'd done it because she didn't know I was the kind of man who would do anything to make her love me. She swallowed, and I wondered if she wanted me to hit her again.

"I'm not that kind of man," I said, and she looked as if she understood.

I went to the dresser for socks. The first week we were married I opened a drawer, and when I saw Nadine's underwear tumbled in with mine I was filled with joy. I was sure the Allies were stronger than the Germans, a belief I wished I could bring myself to share with Nadine as further proof of the kind of man I was, German or not, but all I could do was stare at our jumbled underwear.

I dressed and went to work at Hubig's like I had since 1939.

Walking to the streetcar through a neighborhood that overnight had become less mine, I remembered the Monday morning after Roosevelt died. It'd been only a week and a day since, and I recognized some of the schoolchildren running and yelling in the playground at McDonogh Number 7. That morning they'd been standing silently at the base of the flagpole. Above them the Stars and Stripes hung limply at half-staff. Their teachers were crying and comforting one another, and the kids looked frightened by the adults. I took off my hat, and a little boy watching me took off his cap and elbowed his friend to make him do the same. One of the teachers counted off, and the children began to sing "On-ward Christian Soldiers." That morning everyone at the stop at St. Charles looked as if they had not slept, and as we headed down-town an old man stood beside the conductor offering a rambling eulogy until he couldn't hold back his weeping, at which point each passenger who wasn't sobbing took a turn praising the president. A man who claimed his WPA job building bridges in City Park had kept his children from starving thanked FDR as if he were there to hear it. A girl who looked too young for her nurse's uniform spoke of his kind eyes and blushed. I tried to share their sadness, but "I voted for him four times" was all I could think to say when my turn came. I was ashamed of myself when the bridge-builder turned in his seat to shake my hand. Every flag was lowered and motionless, and the morning sky was funereal gray. At the bakery we greeted each other by mutely shaking our heads. The voice on the radio cataloged the many good things Roosevelt had done for us, and I noted them all, hoping the list would send me bawling into the toi-let like it sent my coworkers, but still my grief didn't match the woe of my fellow citizens. I wondered that day if foreignness was what thinned my sadness. Nadine had fallen to her knees in front of the radio and sobbed prayers the night before, and while she wept, all I'd been able to do was change stations, convinced if I twisted the dial long enough I'd find a voice to tell me there had been a terrible mistake, a cruel hoax, a Nazi rumor. When I couldn't find anyone saying what I wanted to hear, I stopped on a crackling station out of Havana and listened to Latin dance music and static.

A block down Dauphine from the bakery, the wind carried the heavy aroma of sugar, then shifted and was filled with the smoky smell of roasting coffee beans. I stood with eyes closed and sniffed the air.

There was a short guy with a drunk's red nose and a GI haircut examining my timecard when I got to the bakery.

"Schmidt?" he asked when he saw me.

"Yes?" I didn't know him. "Can I help you?"

A snort was his answer. Bert, my foreman, stuck his head from the office door and tipped his head toward the man holding my card. "That's Stanley, my cousin, just out the army."

"*Schmidt*," Stanley muttered.

"I want you to show him around," Bert said.

Stanley followed me through the bakery. He complained about the aprons and paper hats we had to wear—"I look like a faggot," he whined. He complained about the noise of the pie-wrapping machine and the smell of the lard.

I checked the schedule and explained we were going to bake custard pies. "We're lucky to have the eggs," I told him.

"Alleluia," he said. "When's lunch?"

Custard pies are at once simple and tricky. The first step is to slide empty shells into the oven, some of them six feet back. Once the oven is full of shells, each is filled with custard poured from a pot on a pole, the back ones first since those shells have been in the longest. The tricky part is getting an even level in each pie, something not everyone cared about, but I did, and that's why I was most often on the schedule for custard. Anyone could handle apple, and fried pies were simple, no matter the filling.

Stanley watched me fill two shells and started talking. Out of complaints, he turned to boasting. "I get back, I call this girl I went with before—this real whore—and she tells me she's *married*." He snickered at the impossibility and poked me in the ribs, and I filled a pie over its edge. The smell of burning custard came from the oven. "Before I can even say *congratulations* the slut's giving me her new address, and before I can even buy Mrs. McRoundheels a gift, she's sucking my cock." My hands were shaking, and the pies were

44

nowhere near even. Stanley stroked his chin like a philosopher. "Irish girls suck good cock."

I filled the last shell and stepped back from the oven. "My wife's Irish."

He slapped my back. "So you know what I mean?"

"No," I said.

He shrugged. "You Krauts don't like getting your cocks sucked? Hard to believe—your girls seemed to like sucking mine. Makes me feel better about killing your cousins and uncles, put them out of their misery."

I swung the pole, and the custard pot rang against Stanley's head. He fell heavily, the paper hat stayed stuck to his pomaded hair, and he was back on his feet so quickly I could only manage to brandish the pot, not give him another lick.

"*Motherfucker!*" Stanley yelled. He touched his temple and looked at the blood on his fingers. "You Nazi son of a bitch!"

Bert hurried from the office and stood between Stanley and me. He looked at his cousin's bloody head. "Take a walk, Walter."

"Motherfucker!" Stanley hollered again.

"He insulted my wife, my mother, my cousin, my uncle." I felt like a schoolboy explaining myself to a teacher.

A handful of my coworkers came to see what the noise was about. Bert looked over his shoulder and saw them watching. "Take tomorrow off."

Stanley acted as if his cousin was holding him back and yelled, "You motherfucking Nazi son of a bitch!"

"He had it coming," I said. Stanley stepped around Bert, but when I choked up on the pole, ready to hit him again, he backed off.

"Take the week off," Bert said. "Take two. Take three."

"Am I fired?" I asked, astounded.

"Perhaps maybe."

"Perhaps maybe?"

Behind him Stanley hitched up his pants like he was getting ready for the real fight. I watched men I'd worked with for years turning away, pretending they didn't see what was going on. I knew their birthdays, their children's names.

"Fired after six years?"

"Perhaps maybe, *Schmidt*," Bert snapped.

Flabbergasted, I dropped the custard pot. I said to no one and to everyone, "These come out in thirty minutes," then clocked out and walked up Dauphine until my knees shook so badly I thought I would fall. I sat down on someone's front steps.

New Orleans was full of Germans. The neighborhood I sat in taking deep breaths of sugared air was traditionally German. Germans had come into the port for more than a hundred years, like the Irish and the Italians. Maybe we lacked a few of the generations that the French and the Africans could boast, but even the capture of the spy named Schmidt had caused only jokes, not hostility. I was born in Germany, I never denied it, but I'd lived in the United States of America since 1928, and I'd been a naturalized citizen since 1929. In February 1942 I attempted to enlist in both the army and navy but was deemed 4-F because of my dentures.

I couldn't bear to go home, so I headed to Canal Street and spent the day in the cool darkness of Loew's watching an Abbott and Costello double-double feature and eating Hershey's bars. Countless times Nadine had sat between Sammy and me in the same theater, watching the same movies, eating the same candy. That was when I thought she preferred him to me, but then she'd taken my hand on the streetcar. I knew she would say yes when I asked her to marry me, and I thought that was because I'd been wrong about her feelings for Sammy, but sitting in the darkness of the theater I wondered if there was some other reason. Had he rejected her? Was I her second choice? I realized I didn't care. Even if mine was the last name on her list, below both Sammy and dead Bobby, the sour truth was that I loved Nadine and I wanted her to love me.

I thought of the shoebox of Sammy's money, stashed in my toolshed, and again it occurred to me how bizarre it was that he had so much cash. A thousand dollars was more than I'd make in three months at the bakery; if I kept it, I wouldn't have to worry about finding another job or going back to Bert with hat in hand. The war would end and Bert would cool off and apologize, and if he didn't, I'd have plenty of time to find another job. But thinking of the money in that way allowed me to realize something was very, very wrong. I wondered if Sammy had stolen it, or if he'd printed it himself. No milkman had that kind of capital.

I hated him all over again, hated him for sleeping with her, hated him for giving me a thousand dollars. Twice I hadn't done the right thing. I should've killed him when I found him in my bed, I should've killed him when he insulted my wife by putting a price on her. It was too late to fix either mistake. If I killed him, it would look like it took me days to work up the courage. Plotting is not the same as honor. If I gave him back his money, there was still the fact that I'd made the bargain in the first place. Reneging is not the same as honor.

Mixed in with the music of the newsreel's introduction to each of the four films were the jazzy dots and dashes of a Morse code message, and after hearing the message four times, I left the theater with the noise stuck in my head. Onions scented the mild twilight, and for a confused moment I thought I was somehow in Munich; then, as if cued, bright neon buzzed to life along Canal and spelled out English words.

Nadine was frying chicken when I got home. I took the afternoon paper and hid with it in the bathroom. Her locket lay in the soap dish, where she'd set it earlier when she'd bathed. Pots and pans rang in the kitchen, and she hummed a tune, something I hadn't heard her do in weeks. I opened the locket and glared at Bobby's perfect smile and felt foolish for being jealous of a dead man's teeth. I snapped it closed and put it in my pocket.

I unfolded the *Item* and was greeted by a headline about a U-boat sinking an American oil tanker at the mouth of the Mississippi. The Morse code ditty from the newsreel played in my head, and I wished I could recall the language of dots and dashes I'd memorized as a boy. Nadine seemed to be humming the same song.

I opened the paper to its inner pages, unable to bear more war. Every store on Canal had an advertisement for straw hats. A used-kitchen-fats ad proclaimed *There's More War to Come!* and I prayed it wasn't true. I returned the front page and tried to ignore the U-boat and the burning tanker while reading about still-rising flood-waters. War news surrounded the flooding, so I turned to page 7.

There was a small article about a liberated prison camp in which the Nazis had killed as many as twenty thousand people. The article ended, and the gap between it and the advertisement below was filled with the hint *Add carbonated water to fruit punch just before serving it to have the water retain the "sparkle."*

I took the paper to the kitchen. Nadine was standing before the stove stirring string beans, her face flushed and pretty.

"Listen to this," I told her, and then read the article about the camp, paused, and offered the advice about punch.

She shook her head. "That's disgusting."

I wanted her to tell me she knew I too was sickened so I could return to my simple, stupid American guilt and failures. I wanted to be the kind of man who could weep over my dead president, celebrate that the Allies had crossed the Elbe, yell at my wife for getting into bed with my best friend, admit I'd been fired for defending her honor. Why couldn't I do that? What stopped me from at least bragging I'd hit Stanley with a custard pot?

"I got fired," I told her. "A new guy insulted Irish girls, and I hit him in the head with a custard pot."

The half-smile on Nadine's face made her look like she was waiting for the joke's punch line.

I dug into my pocket. "Here," I said, and held out her locket, Bobby safe inside.

◆◆◆

Wednesday morning I told Nadine I was going to look for a new job, but I couldn't bring myself to open the *Picayune* to the employment ads for fear of what else I might find inside, so I caught the Magazine streetcar and wasted the day on Canal listening to records, trying on hats, eating an ice cream cone, drinking a cherry soda. I prayed the war would end abruptly, that in the next shop a crowd would be circled around a radio from which the news of Nazi surrender blared. Instead I found helpful salesgirls offering bargains. Neckties, portable typewriters, sunglasses, cigar cutters, wristwatches on alligator bands: with Sammy's money I could've bought everything they hawked, but my plan was to while away a few hours, go home, get the shoebox, and take it back to him. I considered defecating in the box, atop the money, but decided that was pathetic.

I wondered if he had the nerve to come nosing around while he thought I was at work, either to try to get his money back, or to try to get Nadine to repeat what I'd caught them at, or both. I reminded myself that the kind of man I was trusted her, trusted she was telling the truth when she told me it had been but once, trusted she would never do it again.

I paid for lunch with my own money. In the toy section at D. H. Holmes I bought a Morse code set for the little booklet that translated the alphabet into dots and dashes. The message from the newsreel was still bouncing through my skull, and I hoped I might be able to stop it by learning what it meant, if it meant anything.

On the box lid a vignette in a circle showed a blond soldier tapping a message that a redhead wearing earphones in another circle listened to, pencil poised over pad. Between the two, bombs fell from the belly of a B-29 and exploded in orange starbursts on Gothic rooftops. When the clerk offered to wrap the toy for me, I accepted.

"It's a gift for my son," I lied.

In a voodoo drugstore on Rampart Street I asked a nervous shopkeeper for Fast Luck Drops, a cure one of the bakers at Hubig's swore by when he wasn't winning at craps and needed a change of fortune to pay the rent. I planned to use them to speed the war.

"You the law?" the shopkeeper wanted to know.

I knew his was a business only somewhat legal, less so if he sold charms to whites, and I shook my head. "Nope, Nazi spy," I joked, relieved and stupidly sure I could say whatever I wanted to him because he was black.

He looked me up and down. "Yes sir," he said. "Could be."

I was stunned. Did I look like a spy? Was there a German growl in my vowels? Had someone seen me buy the Morse code set? I hurried out without the drops before he could ask any questions and ducked into the bar next door, where I ordered a shot of rye to ground my flickering nerves. The dozen black men in the room stopped talking when I came in and silently watched me toss back the whiskey. The radio spoke of floodwaters, Roosevelt, the St. Louis Cardinals. I hoped there would be no mention of the war or of Nazis.

A man's voice tight with rage and sadness began to speak of a liberated German camp and the scene he'd witnessed there. He spoke of the smell of the crowd of men and boys who reached out to touch him. "Death had already marked many of them, but they were smiling with their eyes. I looked out over the mass of men to the green fields beyond, where well-fed Germans were plowing."

I felt the unsmiling eyes of every man in the room upon my back, and I was sure they were glaring not because I was a white man in a black bar, but because they could tell I was Hun. The radio voice told of children with numbers tattooed on their arms, the death of thousands of prisoners in a single day from tuberculosis, starvation, fatigue, and the simple loss of the desire to live. Desperate for more whiskey, I waved at the bartender. He ignored me, and the voice described bodies stacked like cordwood, all that was mortal of more than five hundred men and boys.

"If I have offended you by this rather mild account," the voice said, "I'm not in the least sorry."

I counted my steps on the way to the door to keep from bolting.

The crowd on Canal calmed me until I noticed a man in a Panama hat who seemed to be following me, stopping to look into the windows I stopped to look into, turning into Katz's to sip from the water fountain when I did. I lost him by spinning two circuits in a revolving door, but my armpits were sopping and my heart racing.

On the streetcar two men behind me began to discuss troop movements, a propaganda poster unbelievably come to life. They offered their secrets so close to me I could feel their conjoined hot breath on the back of my neck, and I grew convinced they were trying to bait me into jotting notes. I wanted to get off at the next stop, but I feared I'd look suspicious if I did. The rye wasn't keeping my hands from shaking, and to steady them I clenched the package with the Morse code key inside so tightly that I left sweaty prints on the wrapping paper.

I was more exhausted by the time the car reached my stop than I would've been had I worked a double shift at the bakery. Every tree root tripped me as I walked down Milan looking over my shoulder. I fell off the curb and into Constance Street, the Morse code set bouncing into and out of a puddle. I marked its paper with blood when I retrieved it—I'd skinned my palms.

I was turning the knob when from across the street a Zanca hailed me. "Crawfish boil!" one of the daughters yelled. I'd always assumed she was the youngest because she was the shortest. "Come on over!"

"No thank you!" I hollered back, unable to remember her name, if I'd ever known it. "Nadine's waiting for me!"

The daughter shook her head. "She's over here!"

I didn't believe her, but I was too rattled to refuse. I followed her along the side of 729 and in the backyard found Nadine standing amid the gathered clan. She wore a dazed grin and choked the neck of a bottle of Regal with each hand. When she saw me, she held out the beer in her left fist. I drank every lukewarm drop in a single frantic swallow that left me gasping. Nadine laughed uncomfortably, and Dom Zanca slapped me on the back.

"Like your beer, Walter?" he bellowed. "Gee, I know I do!"

I couldn't figure out what was going on; I wanted another bottle.

Bobby's mother pointed to the gift-wrapped box I held. "What's that?"

The festive paper was wrinkled and stained with my bloody fingerprints, the ribbon crushed. I held it out to Nadine. "For you, sweetie pie."

She looked pleased until she opened it. "Thank you," she mumbled, puzzled, and I said as if reminding her, "You wanted to learn Morse code?" She smiled and did her best to play along.

The Zanca boys were impressed by the box top. "Lousy Krauts," one piped, and I had to stop myself from wringing my injured hands.

By the back fence an iron cauldron boiled above an open fire of what appeared to be newspapers and smashed crates, and one of the husbands stirred it with a boat oar. Nadine introduced me to everyone—Sarah, Sally, Sylvia, Steven, Steven. I wasn't sure if she was or wasn't joking when she hissed S after S. For the first time I heard Bobby's married sisters' surnames—Benoit and Berry, their husbands the pair of Stevens. I'd thought of them all as Zancas for so long that their real names sounded fake.

The girl child, once Nadine's niece, was Holly, and the former nephews were Billy and Willy and Arty. Holly, all of five years old, brought me another beer from an ice chest and took my empty. The chilled glass felt good against my injured palms, and when I put the bottle to my lips, I could feel cold beer trickling down my throat and slowing my heart. The boys were taunting the crawfish, poking at the bag with sticks, daring each other to put a fingertip inside a claw and pretending the pinch was painless to get Arty, the baby, to do it. He wailed, and while the child was soothed and mocked by his extended family, I whispered into Nadine's ear, "These people wouldn't even talk to you yesterday."

She sipped her Regal and wouldn't look me in the eye. "Things change," she explained. "I like the toy." She rattled the box, clearly hoping there was something better inside than what the lid promised. "It's the thought that counts," she assured me.

Before I could ask her to explain more exactly what things had changed, Dom Zanca told me he wanted to show me something in his toolshed. The little building stank of gasoline and mildew; there was nothing for him to show me. The old man stood at the dirty window watching his grandchildren and great-grandchildren.

"They miss they daddy."

I looked over his shoulder and wondered whom he was talking about. The four little kids had joined hands and were dancing around Nadine.

"War took him, too."

I watched Nadine's face tighten and knew she was about to cry, and I shared her sadness with the clarity of feeling someone else's pain that only true love allows.

"Elroy," the old man said.

Nadine was weeping, and I drank to keep myself from joining her. The children quit dancing. Quickly their mothers formed a new circle to comfort her. Nadine stood in sunlight, but rain rattled on the shed's metal roof.

"Devil's beating his wife," Dom Zanca said, and I gagged on a sip of beer. They were being nice to Nadine because she told them I'd hit her. I realized how odd the Morse code set looked as a husband's apology for a slap.

"We say that when it's raining while the sun's shining." Fat silver drops fell glittering from a clear blue sky as if to illustrate his explanation. He pointed. "Devil's beating his wife."

They didn't know I'd hit her.

I wanted to go to Nadine, but I knew what she wanted was the attention of her lost sisters-in-law, the beer little Holly handed her, the plate of crawfish her one-time brother-in-law brought.

"Them Hubee's is good pics," Dom Zanca said. "Willy's Wilbur and Billy's William." He sighed. "That river's still rising." His small talk was so mechanical I didn't bother to respond. A long shelf ran the length of the shed, clear glass oyster jars filled with screws and nuts hanging from its underside, their lids nailed to the shelf's bottom. The old man twisted off a jar of bolts and shook it.

"I lost two boys to this war, Bobby and Bobby's daddy—Elroy." He poured the bolts onto the dirt floor and cranked the empty jar back onto its lid. "They *took* my two boys," he corrected, then kicked the bolts into the corner. I thought of my own father, taken in the last war. "Took my boys and left me *that*." He pointed to his laughing sons-in-law.

Nadine was eating crawfish, and I longed to sit beside her and watch her fingers disassemble one of the little monsters, crack off its head, split its shell, bite down on the white tail meat with its pink pinstripe. I wanted to kiss her spicy lips.

"I got bills to pay and no son to help me, no grandson neither," Dom Zanca told me. "Nadine says you come into some money and you'll help me out." He shrugged. "You and me's almost like family, almost. We got sweet, kind Nadine in common."

Sweet, kind Nadine had found Sammy's shoebox. I looked at her and wondered if she'd figured out where the money had come from before she offered it to people who just yesterday had treated her so meanly.

"How about a thousand dollars?" I asked the old man.

He stuck out his hand, and when I took it, he crushed my knuckles until I nearly screamed.

"Call me Poppa Dom," he instructed.

A fat raindrop smacked my forehead like a sloppy kiss when I followed Poppa Dom from the shed. Nadine begged me with her eyes, and I bent and kissed her wetly as a raindrop.

"Mild spring, big mudbugs," Poppa Dom proclaimed, happy and loud.

I sprinted across the street, counted fifties and twenties to make sure Sammy hadn't lied, wrapped the bills in a crazed sheet of tinfoil that'd been used and reused many times, and ran back. Poppa Dom smelled the package as if I'd brought him a big piece of fudge.

"You a good man," he said, then slapped my back.

I wanted to convince myself that giving him the money so Nadine could be happy was like being allowed a second chance to refuse Sammy's offer, but it was impossible to make that logic work. Instead I watched Nadine grin, listened to the Zancas laugh at her jokes, and tried not think of logic, or of what it meant that I'd spent all of Sammy's cash bribing dead Bobby's grandpa to be nice to my wife.

The days were growing longer. When the crawfish and beer were gone and we returned to our little house, the bedroom curtains were still full of the last of the sunset. We drunkenly waltzed from room to room, hugging for balance while we groped each other. Nadine's salt and pepper shakers jumped when we bounced against the curio cabinet. When we slid along the wall, the framed faces of her mother and father were close enough to kiss. We climbed into bed still half-dressed, Nadine's skirt up around her waist, my pants twisted around one ankle. We were frantic and laughing and clumsy like kids looped on lust, not man and wife boozed on beer.

Each of us breathed in the spent air the other gasped out, and I grew lightheaded as her panting rose from alto to soprano. I forgave her everything—cuckolding, calling me *Kraut*, buying kindness from the Zancas.

I lay beside her afterward, unable to join her in the sleep into which she quickly and deeply tumbled. I watched the ceiling and remembered how my thoughts had kept me awake when I was a child, how after hours of studying the crack across my boyhood ceiling—river on a snow map, black lightning bolt across a white sky—I began hearing the words inside the schoolbooks stacked on my desk, and I rose, opened their covers and listened, checking the window for dawn after each page so I could put out the lamp and hurry into bed and trick my mother into thinking I'd been asleep.

Thunder rattled the windowpanes and woke me. The luminous clockface showed it was long past midnight in New Orleans. I got up to lower the sashes. Voices murmured like my schoolbooks used to, Zancas up late gossiping on the telephone, maybe a radio left on when everyone but me was asleep.

I woke in rainy-day morning darkness from a dream in which I sipped coffee across the kitchen table from Nadine and watched the rain smear the window's green view of the banana trees while she read *Life* and ate her toast—a normalcy now impossible to manage while awake. It seemed unlikely we wouldn't discuss the money, so before Nadine woke, I slipped out of bed, dressed, put on my raincoat, opened my umbrella, and stepped into the storm.

A Mercury coupe with the ugly wooden bumpers wartime cars suffered because of rationed chrome and steel idled at the corner of Milan and Magazine. When I came up beside it, the driver's window rolled down and Sammy blew a cloud of smoke into the rain and asked, "What's the good word?"

I circled the car, closed my umbrella, and opened the passenger door. The crossing guard was inside, his yellow slicker shiny with rain. He held his stop sign in front of himself like a shield. "Monday," he begged in a wobbling voice.

Water ran down my neck while I stood in the street waiting for him to get out. I opened my umbrella back up. Two little girls in matching flowered rain bonnets stood at the corner looking for the guard, holding hands, too afraid to cross without help.

"Fuck Monday," Sammy said.

"Sunday?" the crossing guard suggested.

Sammy punched his stop sign and left a deep dent in the tin. He was wearing brass knuckles, and he held his fist under the man's nose. "Tomorrow," he told him.

The crossing guard sucked in the kind of quick, deep breath that usually comes out as sobbing, but he held it and got out. The little girls jumped up and down when he stepped into Magazine and raised his dented sign.

Sammy turned the key and I got in and closed the door. He pulled away from the curb while he shook the brass knuckles off his fingers. "Tomorrow!" he yelled through the glass at the cringing man. He tucked the knuckles into his breast pocket as easily as he would a pack of cigarettes.

I peeked at the odometer and saw mostly zeros. "Whose car is this?"

"The answer to that question is *Mind your own goddamn business*."

The rain intensified, and I couldn't see anything except blurred brake lights and the dim colors of traffic signals. Sammy made a few turns, and I guessed we were on Tchoupitoulas, but I couldn't tell if we were heading downtown or up.

He was a jerk, he'd always been a jerk, and I was surprised how happy I was to see him. I was still hurt by his betrayal, but he was— or at least he had been—my best friend. When he'd invited me to join him and Nadine in that booth at Katz's, he'd not only introduced me to the woman who would become my wife, but he'd taught me, by example, how to be an American. I'd witnessed his boldness, his shameless desire to become something else, something better; I'd studied his unwavering belief that he would, sooner rather than later, be that richer, thinner, more handsome, and more beloved man, no matter what he was before. Imagine how learning to believe this about myself lifted me. Imagine how doubting this faith broke me.

I wanted to tell my best friend I'd been fired for defending Nadine's honor and have my best friend tell me I was right to do what I'd done. Sammy knew all about the Zancas, and I wanted to tell him I'd paid Poppa Dom so the lot of them would be nice to Nadine and have Sammy tell me he would've done the same. I wanted to tell him I was unable to cry about Roosevelt, wanted to apologize for the suffering my countrymen had caused, and I wanted him to tell me he understood and didn't blame me, didn't even consider me German.

"I need that money," he said before I could figure out where to begin. "Wasn't mine to give you."

I stared at his profile, amazed by what an asshole he was. "It's gone," I told him. "I spent every penny."

He groaned. "I thought you were my friend."

"Your friend?" I shouted. "You thought I was your *friend*?"

"Yes!" he yelled back. He blew the horn at the storm and said nothing more.

Rain snapped off the windshield loudly as hail. "Whose money was it?"

He shrugged. "Bookmaker I work for."

"You told me you worked for Brown's Velvet, delivering milk."

He shrugged again. "And you told me you worked for Hubig's, making pies, but I know that's not true—anymore." He didn't take his eyes off the road, but he smirked as if he'd seen me flinch. "I got my ways," he said, then snorted. "People's betting on the flood: when the levees will break, how far upriver, how many cows drown, how many sandbag-stacking Kraut POWs go missing." He turned onto Magazine, and I knew we were heading Uptown. "You can bet on damn near anything. Wish I'd put money on you getting canned."

"Where're we going?" I demanded.

Sammy wiped the windshield with his elbow. "How about that Roosevelt? I thought that gimp son-of-a-bitch was never going to die. Would've got unbelievable odds if I'd thought to bet on that a year or so ago."

My mouth went dry. I wondered if he could read my mind, and next he'd mock me for paying Poppa Dom to be nice to Nadine. We passed the zoo, and the levee rose before us. I imagined a fissure zigzagging down it and brown water pouring through. Sammy kept looking in the rearview, but when I turned my head the Mercury's back window was fogged white as milk glass. While I was twisted in my seat he swerved into the open doors of a small, empty warehouse. The noise of the rain on the Mercury's windshield was replaced by the roar of the downpour on the building's tin roof.

Sammy covered his mouth and rasped, "Play along," then opened the door.

Deep in the shadows, a brand-new Packard with chrome bumpers purred and puffed exhaust. Its wet tire tracks crisscrossed the floor. The man behind the wheel looked so much like my former fellow roomer Edward the librarian that I had to swallow a greeting.

"Stewart, what's the good word?" Sammy sang. He pointed to me. "My brother," he told the man. The rain and wind rattled the tin so violently he had to yell. "His wife's who's sick."

I rubbed my temples in theatrical anguish, then realized Stewart was the bookmaker and my fictional sick wife was Sammy's excuse. At that moment it would've been easy to betray Sammy, and I'll never be sure why I didn't—residue of friendship, fear the man in the car would hurt me too—but I didn't.

Stewart yelled back, "I came here for my money, not to meet your kin!" His voice was nothing like Edward's. "Pray that river takes its sweet time rising, Sammy. Pray you get my money before I got to pay somebody." He rolled up his window and put the beautiful car in gear while Sammy politely knocked on the glass.

"She's got *female* troubles!" he pleaded.

The downpour erased the Packard like a magic trick.

"Female troubles?" I said.

"Fuck you," he answered. I watched him slip his hand into his pocket and looked around for something to use to defend myself against brass knuckles. A piece of two-by-four was a few feet away. Sammy brought out a pack of Lucky Strikes and put one between his lips, where it jiggled until it fell from his mouth before he could light it. He tossed down the unstruck match and barked again,

"Fuck you." I didn't follow when he got into the car, and he didn't wait for me before driving into the rain.

I went to the open end of the warehouse and closed my eyes and felt the storm's hot, wet breath on my face. The din cleared my head of worry, and it was only when it abruptly stopped and I opened my eyes to find the sun burning a hole through the last of the clouds that I began to fret. Across the street, on the porch of a tidy barge-board house that had been obscured by the deluge, an old black man sat watching me. A sunbeam stabbed a puddle at my feet.

"Devil's beating his wife," I called, my voice too loud in the new silence.

"That's it," he agreed.

Birds began to chitter; a dog barked happily. Wadded-paper thunderheads hung over the Mississippi. I crossed Leake Avenue and climbed the levee. Muddy water lapped at the sandbags top-ping it—I wondered if German POWs had stacked them—and when I turned away from the river, I saw I stood higher than the roofs of the houses below. The man on the porch waved and yelled something I couldn't understand.

"That's it!" I yelled back.

He and his shack would be submerged if the levee gave. My own house, on higher ground, would be flooded to its eaves. I knew from the paper and the radio that it was still raining in Missouri and Illinois and the snow was melting up in Minnesota.

I wondered if Sammy had gone to my house to see if I'd been lying about spending all the money, wondered if Nadine would give him the empty shoebox. I hoped she wouldn't even answer his knock. It was Sammy's fault our friendship was ruined, his fault he'd offered me the money, even his fault I'd hit my foreman's cousin and been fired. I kicked at a sandbag, and a thin trickle of brown water ran over my foot. I wanted the river to ruin Sammy, even if it killed half the residents of New Orleans. I kicked again.

A car horn blew behind me, and I turned. "Quit!" Sammy hollered. "Too many bets on today."

I was running down the levee before I could think. I wasn't sure if I was running to hug him or choke him. I slid into the Mercury knee- and elbow-first, and my funny bone flamed.

Sammy got out of the car and came around to examine the fender. "I need to hide out," he said. "It's not safe for me to go home." His voice cracked with genuine fear. I thought of Stewart's threat, and something inside me fought the twinge of sympathy I was feeling.

"Nadine's pregnant," I fibbed reflexively, and the surprise on his face matched the surprise in my chest.

"Where'd you get this car?" I asked as we turned onto St. Charles. "Test drive." He shot his cuffs to show me his bare wrists. "Had to leave my watch." We rode in silence past Tulane, past the grand homes of cotton barons and sugar kings, past black nannies pushing perambulators. The live oaks were wet and glowing. I rolled down the window and like a dog stuck my head out into the thick air. I was confused. I hated and loved Sammy equally; I wanted as much to save him as to damn him.

The car lot was above Lee Circle, just off the avenue on Melpomene. A short man in a double-breasted jacket came from between two Fords yelling Sammy's name when we parked.

"O'Banion, you shitheel," the little man shrieked. "I been waiting on you for two hours. You were supposed to take it around the block, not up to Memphis."

Sammy cringed and looked around as if killers were already hunting him.

I heard something in the salesman's vowels and stuck my finger into his chest. "You're a Kraut, ain't you?" I said, drawling like a Zanca.

He recoiled and raised his hands.

Sammy was bobbing his head excitedly. "Name's Klaus, or *Adolf,* or something."

"My name's Rudolph," he argued. "My *last* name."

I poked him again. "Listen, *Adolf,* you better give the man his watch."

"I'm an American," he told me indignantly, and I started to lose my nerve.

Sammy slapped my back. "*This* man is an American."

I was nearly overwhelmed by friendship and self-loathing.

"Give him the watch," I said. "*Schnell.*"

Rudolph couldn't get the watch out of his pocket fast enough.

Sammy laughed as we walked to the streetcar stop, laughed when I ignored the conductor and left him to pay for both of us, laughed as the car bounced along past churches and corner groceries and ruined mansions with weak neon signs flickering ROOMS.

"Where the hell did that come from?" he asked when he finally ran out of laughter.

I didn't turn away from my view of the truck full of bricks keeping pace with the streetcar. "Germany," I said.

When I peeked over at him a few blocks later, Sammy was rubbing his palms on his knees and looking over his shoulder to see who was sitting behind us. He flipped up his jacket collar and pulled down his hat brim.

"Maybe the levees will hold," I said.

Sammy sighed. "More bets on that than on them breaking."

I knew a loyal friend would find a way to replace the thousand dollars—but then there was also the fact that a loyal friend wouldn't sleep with his loyal friend's wife.

"How could you?" I asked him.

Sammy peered out from under his hat. "I've made some mistakes," he said pitifully. "But I loved her when she was ugly."

I was so disgusted I could barely keep my voice down. "You have to do what I tell you to do and say what I tell you to say or I'll make sure Stewart finds out what you used his money for." My threat had one significant flaw—I had no idea how to find the bookie who looked like Edward the librarian, or if Stewart was the man's first or last name—but I gambled Sammy was too spooked to consider this, and I was right.

He shrugged. "I don't guess I have a choice in the matter."

Nadine retreated behind a chair when we came into the kitchen through the back door.

"What's the good word?" Sammy asked her.

"Tell her," I said.

He looked at the floor. "Don't love you, never loved you."

I watched Nadine, hoping both she would and wouldn't be hurt. One corner of her mouth twitched twice—up, down—and she nodded as if Sammy had answered a question she'd been afraid to ask.

We three stood for a moment, and then Sammy said, "I'm going to the shed."

I stood beside Nadine, and through the window above the sink we watched Sammy cross our postage-stamp backyard.

"Take him a pillow," she told me, then touched my cheek with her lips.

"That money in the shoebox was his," I said.

She looked away. "I figured."

"I shouldn't have taken it from him."

"Thank you for hitting the guy who insulted Irish girls," she said very formally. She twisted her dishtowel in her hands and asked, "Coffee?"

I thought of her asking the same question the day she took me back to her little house on Conery. "Yes, please," I said. She opened a cupboard. "I love you," I told her.

"I'm sorry," she said, staring at coffee mugs and juice glasses. "I'm so sorry."

I prayed she was apologizing for what she'd done, not bemoaning my love for her. I touched her elbow.

"I'll take him a pillow," I said.

I was peeved to find Sammy had already made himself comfortable. He'd unfolded a cot and was lying on it, listening to a radio I'd bought at a rummage sale and never managed to fix. He had it tuned to a station out of Lafayette. The Cajun on the radio gibbered in backwoods French and then barked, "Plenty whiskey!" through the static before Sammy could sit up and twist down the volume. "Loose tube was all," he told me in his schoolteacher's voice, and before he could lecture me, I reminded him, "You're supposed to be *hiding*."

His face went white. "Didn't think about that."

I held out the pillow, and he took it and hugged it tightly. The Cajun station's signal grew suddenly stronger, and an accordion blared until Sammy turned the radio off.

"Be quiet," I told him, then turned and left.

Nadine was sitting at the kitchen table crying. "What's wrong?" I asked stupidly. What wasn't wrong?

She blew her nose. "I'm pregnant," she whispered.

"What's that?" I was sure I'd misheard.

"I'm pregnant."

The lie I'd told Sammy had come true. "I love you," I told her, too excited to find other words.

"I want to be sure you love me," Nadine said. "I want to be *sure*."

I chased her into the bedroom. I kissed her belly and imagined it swelling. I blew a raspberry on her bellybutton, and Nadine laughed so hard she began to hiccup. She kept hiccupping while we slammed the bed against the wall, bit each other's necks, and ended up trapped inside twisted sheets like lunatics belted into straitjackets.

"Oh my," Nadine said when she caught her breath, and I laughed.

It was still light out when she fell asleep, and I lay beside her and thought about Sammy holed up in the shed. When I considered all the years I'd spent alone, it was hard not to forgive him for what he'd done. He hadn't been wrong when he'd told me over and over I had him to thank for Nadine. If he hadn't called us together that day in the soda fountain, I wouldn't have been lying happily beside my pregnant wife. It occurred to me that there was something nearly chivalrous about his wearing a prophylactic: no question of bloodline. It then occurred to me this was all bullshit and he was no more than a jerk.

◆◆◆

I could still hear the newspaper boy whistling what sounded like the Morse code tune from the newsreel when I took Dom Zanca's *Picayune.* I left its rubber band behind to show him I had—a thousand dollars bought more than a crawfish boil and the right to call him Poppa. I sat on my own steps and read. On the front page was a picture of German POWs raising the levee upriver in Pineville. A small item below announced that henceforth prisoners would be given only hearts, livers, and kidneys, and in order to conserve white flour, their bread would be rye. I was happy to see the daily map of Europe showed spectacular Allied gains. It was captioned "The Squeeze Is Getting Tighter All the Time," and showed a narrowing ribbon of Germany with a half-dozen little American flags to the west and just as many hammers and sickles to the east.

The Mississippi was still rising, but the levees were holding. Near Berlin a ten-year-old boy had asked an American soldier for candy, then pulled a pistol and killed him. There was no mention of what became of the child. In New Orleans three longshoremen had been arrested on the Robin Street wharf unloading a crate of marijuana off a boat from Cuba. The police had donned their summer uniforms.

On page 3 was a report of Nazi guards burning to death more than a thousand prisoners to prevent their rescue by the advancing Americans. The sole survivor reported that the guards soaked straw with gasoline and herded in the victims. The half-inch of leftover column space was filled with "Harrisburg, PA: Mrs. Edwards Martin, Pennsylvania's first lady, has delved into hidden corners of the executive mansion and the statehouse for things to redecorate the Governor's sixty-five-year-old home."

I hated the typesetter; I wished Mrs. Edwards Martin ill. As an American, was I supposed to care equally that the first lady of Pennsylvania had found stashed antiques and that eleven hundred people had been incinerated? I turned to the sports page, but reading the "Baseball Barometer" felt perverted. I wondered if that feeling proved I wasn't fully American: Roosevelt's letter to Kenesaw Mountain Landis made it clear baseball was a good thing, a necessary thing.

It was still hard for me to believe Nadine was pregnant. Perhaps if I hadn't been lying to Sammy when I told him she was, her happy news wouldn't have seemed impossible. Though I had plenty of incentive to hate him, the fact that he'd stolen from me the pure joy of learning that Nadine and I had conjured a baby seemed the best reason to despise Sammy. No matter his troubles, and no matter my involvement in those troubles, I wanted him out of my shed and out of our lives. I had a little more than two hundred dollars in savings, and I decided I'd take out a loan on the house to make up the other eight.

He was lying fully dressed on the camp cot. The shadows under his eyes evidenced a sleepless night.

"Listen," he whispered before I could tell him I would get his money as soon as I could. "I been up all night thinking, and I got to tell the truth. I been lying to you for a long time. I used to pick pockets at the movies. Once I even picked yours."

I remembered the billfold I'd thought I lost a few weeks before I met Nadine and Sammy.

He yawned so widely his jaw popped. "First I wore a navy uniform. Nobody thinks a sailor's a pickpocket. I'd take a wallet, and the mark would run up to me and ask, 'Hey, sailor, seen anybody suspicious?' Cops aren't as dumb as you'd think, though, and in the end one of them figured me—or somebody fingered me. I was in

Orleans Parish Prison for a month. The worst part was the food. I was so hungry that when I got out I spent every dime I had on po-boys and red beans, and I ended up with a new disguise. Turns out a fat man looks innocent as a sailor, more innocent even. I was going good, but there were a couple of times when it was close. Then one day I saw you and Nadine in KB's and thought, 'Three lardasses would look even more innocent than one lardass.'"

I was flabbergasted and hurt. "You used us as a disguise?"

Sammy grinned as if he thought I was impressed. "The diet too."

"What?"

"Sailor, fat man, fat man with his fat friends, skinny guy with his pal and his girl—you've got to keep changing your camouflage. You know, 'cutpurse' is another word for pickpocket, and so is 'dip.'"

I thought of the way Nadine had once nodded and smiled while he went on like this about monkeys or what the Latin mottoes on school crests meant.

"And you can't just wear a big hat." He rubbed his chin. "Maybe I'll grow a beard and dye it and my hair gray, walk stooped over, use a cane."

"Where do the bets on the flood fit into this?"

The joy that had been sparking in Sammy's eyes dimmed. "I'm no fool," he said sharply. "Can't be a pickpocket forever. People put a dollar on a horse, on a ballgame, on when a missing POW's going to get caught by the MPs, on when the Mississippi's going to drown a hundred head of cattle. Those little bets add up. Pretty soon you're driving a new Packard."

He drank from a mug of steaming coffee.

"Where did you get that?" I demanded, worried Nadine had brought it.

He winked. "Girl next door was getting mighty friendly over the fence this morning. Gave me this and a doughnut."

He was talking about the shortest Zanca, Sylvia Benoit. He licked his lips, and I wanted to stab pruning shears into his whorish heart.

"You're supposed to be hiding out," I reminded him. "I hope she doesn't know Stewart." I turned away from his failing smirk and slammed the shed door behind me.

Behind the thin curtain over the kitchen window, Nadine measured grounds into the percolator. Soon she would fry me an egg. I took a deep breath and decided to go for a walk to clear my head.

Sylvia saw me coming along the path between my narrow house and hers before I saw her.

"We didn't believe your story," she hissed from behind a gardenia bush. "We believed your hundred dollars."

"What?" I asked, confused but ready to remind her it was a *thou sand* dollars I'd given her grandfather, not a hundred, and didn't that prove something about my story?

Sylvia stood up and looked over her shoulder, then turned back to me. "You know, you don't have to act with me, Steve. You don't have to say anything and you don't have to do anything—not a thing. Oh, maybe just whistle. You know how to whistle, don't you, Steve? You just put your lips together—and *blow*."

Her husband's name was Steven. "Are you all right?" I asked. "It's me, Walt, not Steven."

She puckered, closed her eyes, and turned up her face as if she wanted me to kiss her. When I didn't, she squinted at me and frowned. "Are you afraid to get married or something?" she sassed, and suddenly Sylvia's non sequiturs made sense: She was reciting lines from movies. I recognized the last from *The More the Merrier.*

She picked a gardenia and sniffed it. "Are you getting ritzy with me?" she piped. *Sullivan's Travels.* The others were from *To Have and Have Not* and *The Maltese Falcon.* I felt a glimmer of pride for being able to identify her sources, then ashamed for spending years sitting in the dark watching movies.

"I'm no good at being noble, but it doesn't take much to see that the problems of three little people don't amount to a hill of beans in this crazy world. Someday you'll understand that—not now. Here's looking at you, kid." She held out the gardenia, and I took it.

She delivered her lines so earnestly and naturally—it didn't matter that half of them originally came from the mouths of men—that I almost asked her to explain herself. Three little people? Me, Nadine, and Sammy?

"Is that a banana in your pocket, or are you happy to see me?"

"Goodness!" I supplied.

She was delighted. "Goodness has nothing to do with it!"

"Sylvia, you need to stay away from that man in the shed."

"Why Hopsie, you ought to be kept in a cage!"

The Lady Eve, Barbara Stanwyck. How many movies had I seen? How many had Sylvia seen? "Where's your husband?" I asked, and as I had hoped, that ruined her fun.

She sighed. "Went up to Alexandria to sell hicks something they don't need." A crash and a yelp came from the house, and she went to attend to her children. Walking away, she shimmied like Bacall in *To Have and Have Not*. "Blow!" she called over her shoulder.

When I came around the corner of the house, I saw Poppa Dom standing on his porch, stretching on his thumb and first finger the rubber band I'd left behind.

"Morning," he hailed, and kept stretching the rubber band. I wondered what he would do and how mean the Zancas would be to Nadine if I asked him to give me the money back.

"That fellow sleeping in your shed looks familiar," he said.

I felt my ears redden. "Friend of mine down on his luck."

Poppa Dom nodded. "My grandson loved that girl. Bobby was a damn dog, stupid and mean sometimes, but he loved her. She was too good for him—even his momma them'll admit it—but Nadine loved him back." He hitched up his pants and cleared his throat. "She been hurt too much. Don't hurt her." It was an odd lecture coming from the man I'd had to pay to be nice to her.

I wanted to escape all the weirdness. "Can I borrow your car?" I asked, sure he'd say no.

"Key's in the ashtray."

I felt bad for stealing his newspaper. After I'd read it, I'd folded it and tucked it between the empty milk bottles in the Brown's box, and I took it out and walked over to his porch. "I think the boy tossed your paper on my porch."

He fitted the rubber band around it.

I was surprised how smoothly the rattletrap Plymouth turned over. There was a new radio in the dash tuned to the Cajun station Sammy liked. I turned it off and pulled away from the curb. A few blocks along it occurred to me the new radio was probably paid for with some of Sammy's loot. I turned it on despite its origin. I needed some noise to stop the thoughts of Nazis and Pennsylvania's First Lady and Sammy's numerous betrayals.

A woman was lamenting something to the accompaniment of an accordion when I stopped at a red light at the corner of Magazine and Jackson. A group of POWs lackadaisically filled a pothole. One of the men leaned on his shovel and looked in my direction. He said something to me, but the radio was too loud, and then the car behind me was honking—the light had turned green—and I instinctively pressed the gas. I pulled over in the next block and closed my eyes. I was sure it had been Andreas.

I threw the Plymouth into gear, stalled it, nearly flooded the engine, and raced through the three right turns it took to make the block. I parked the car and stood on the filled pothole. The POWs were gone, the sticky black patch of asphalt the only proof I hadn't been hallucinating. I shaded my eyes and looked up then down Jackson, but the truck was nowhere to be seen. The POW's hair was duller than Andreas's blond had been, but my brown was threaded with gray. His pale blue eyes, his Roman nose, his long arms and girlish wrists—I couldn't tell if I had seen these things when I looked at the POW or if I was simply remembering my cousin.

I took a deep breath and told myself I was imagining things. Thin wrists and what was probably an obscenity didn't prove anything beyond the fact that my wife was pregnant, I'd caught her in bed with my best friend, and he was hiding in my toolshed because I'd given away a shoebox of his bookie boss's money. My hands were shaking when I got back into the Plymouth, and I considered a drink, then settled for a bottle of Coke from the filling station.

Nadine was in the kitchen. "Two men came to the door asking for Sammy," she said. She described Stewart and what sounded like a goon from a gangster picture. "They acted like they knew I was lying when I told them I hadn't seen him in days."

For the first time it became clear to me we were in trouble too. "Do we have any beer?" I asked.

She opened the Frigidaire and handed me a bottle of Jax. "He gave you that money to try and make things right, right?"

"He used us as a disguise," I told her.

"I don't know what that means."

"When we were all fat, he figured out if we went around in a group, no one would suspect him—he's a pickpocket. He even got us to go on a diet because he needed to change his disguise."

She pursed her lips into a tight bud, and it looked like she was going to cry. "I wish you'd killed him," she said.

"I have to think for a little while," I told her, and took the bottle into the bathroom. I sat on the edge of the tub and sipped cold beer and tried to slow my racing brain. Nadine's wish that I'd killed Sammy stuck me as insincere, something an actress would say in a gangster film, and I wondered if she'd said it because she thought I wanted to hear it, not because she really wished him dead by my hand.

Out the window I heard Sammy's voice, but I couldn't make out any words.

"Why Hopsie, you ought to be kept in a cage!" Sylvia bubbled.

He was too flirtatious to hide. I remembered the terror in Sammy's eyes in the warehouse, the way he kept looking over his shoulder on the streetcar. Stewart would be back, and I worried that when he came, he would hurt Nadine, the baby-to-be, and me. It even occurred to me Sammy might want that to happen. There was no way for me to win. Giving Poppa Dom the money to be nice to her had put Nadine and the baby in harm's way.

Nadine rapped on the door. "You all right?" She turned the knob and came in.

"That man who came looking for him is a bookie, and the money Sammy gave me is his, and when Sammy can't give it back, we're all going to be in danger."

"Florida," she told me. "Esther. My sister."

I recalled the postcards she'd once shown me, but this was the first time I'd heard her sister's name.

I thought of Sammy asking me what the good word was while he pulled up his pants, thought about how selfish and vain he was, so selfish and vain he couldn't even bring himself to lay low. I did my best to convince myself leaving him to face his punishment wouldn't mean I'd done something wrong, but I couldn't.

"We have to take Sammy with us," I told Nadine. "Maybe Poppa Dom will lend us his car."

She took in a long breath through her nose, let it out slowly. "Is anyone's life simple?" she wondered.

Sammy agreed so enthusiastically that I knew without a doubt Stewart wouldn't single Sammy out for punishment when he came to collect. Nadine asked Poppa Dom if we could borrow his car for a trip, and he said yes and gave her his gasoline ration book, no questions asked. I was spooked enough to demand we wait until after midnight before we made our getaway. While we waited, I paced, and the dots and dashes of Morse code began again. I transcribed what I heard onto the back of the light bill's envelope, found the toy set on a shelf in the salt-shaker cabinet, then used the little booklet to translate. It was gibberish, and as soon as I saw the mess of vowels and consonants, the noise in my head vanished.

We rode in silence, and I watched Sammy in the rearview and Nadine from the corner of my eye, looking for signs she felt for him something she didn't feel for me, or that Sammy wanted more from her than a roll in the sheets. I wanted to see in a wink or a smile or a nod proof Nadine had chosen me and was happy with her choice, that she would've chosen me over Bobby if she'd had the chance. I had to settle for not seeing any evidence to the contrary.

The road along the Gulf of Mexico had identical shacks every two or three miles, each with a sign that promised BEER FISH WHISKEY. Nadine slept against the door; Sammy snored in the back. The farther into the empty night we traveled, the less crowded the radio dial became, until I was alone with a single station out of Tallahassee. The announcer was reading the newspaper, and I listened to him describe the funnies. He changed his voice for each cartoon character and laughed softly at their harmless punch lines.

It was almost noon when Nadine had me turn down a shell road. Patches of grass looked like scabs on the low dunes. Sammy was asleep behind us. My eyes felt like someone had kicked sand in my face, and my bladder was full of the Coca-Cola I'd been drinking to stay awake. I rolled down the window, and the smell of the Gulf was so strong I could taste salt.

Over the next dune stood four outhouses. One more dune, and the view opened to the Gulf of Mexico, gilded by sun. A row of small cottages faced the golden surf, one for each outhouse. Nadine pointed to the first in line, and I parked beside it. Her sister wasn't home, but Nadine told us Esther kept a key hidden in the privy, and she went to fetch it. I watched her hurry across the sand. Sammy peeked between the plank shutters, then went to the next cottage in the row and peeked between its shutters, then moved on to the third. I kicked off my shoes, pulled off my socks, and walked to the water's edge, listened to the slap and hiss of the waves, then stepped into the Gulf. It was my first time in an ocean. It was warmer than I'd expected.

"Ghost town!" Sammy yelled from the little front porch of the fourth cottage. He jogged down the sand while I rolled my cuffs and waded.

"I'll be dogcatcher." His voice was filled with manic delight. "You want to be mayor?"

A wave broke over the tops of his shoes, and he looked down at his feet but did not move, even when another, larger wave covered them.

"I'm so tired," he said, his voice emptied of excitement. His pants were wet almost to his knees. "I've got only the one pair of shoes, and these are my only trousers."

Over his shoulder Nadine was waving.

"She found the key," I told him.

Nadine opened the storm shutters and the windows and gave us the tour. The cottage was three rooms deep—parlor, kitchen, bedroom. When Sammy realized he was leaving wet footprints, he took off his shoes and threw them out the front door, then slumped onto the couch and sat with his eyes closed.

"What the hell is wrong with me?" he groaned.

"We're all tired," I said, even though Sammy and Nadine had slept for most of the drive.

In the bedroom Nadine and I lay, our noses only a few inches apart, on a narrow mattress that smelled of mildew and salt. When she told me, "These were once honeymoon cottages," I thought she was flirting, but when I put my hand under her slip, she squeezed shut her legs and said, "Sammy." I jerked my hand free and wondered if she felt some kind of lover's loyalty to Sammy even if she claimed she wished I'd killed him.

"Let's go swimming," she said.

Nadine loved Pontchartrain Beach and the pool at Audubon Park, so I shouldn't have been surprised she'd packed my trunks, something I wouldn't have thought to do—I'd considered Florida solely a hideout. She turned her back to undress, but I'd suffered enough modesty. When she pulled her slip over her head, I reached under her arms and held her breasts. She looked over her shoulder and grinned. I slid one hand down onto her belly and felt its slight rise, unable to tell if there was yet any difference.

"Later," she promised, and I let her go and watched her tug up the striped second skin of the bottom of her swimsuit, then pull its top down over her chest.

"Hurry up," she told me. "I'll meet you in the water."

The screen door that led out back slapped shut behind her. I watched her walk up the dune that hid the outhouses. When she disappeared, I got into my trunks and opened the door to the kitchen. Sammy was stripped to the waist, holding a hand mirror so he could see the reflection of his back in a mirror on the wall of the front room. Bruises covered his body, dark and lurid as a sailor's tattoos. When Stewart had threatened Sammy, I thought it was all talk, Sammy's enemies as full of shit as he was, but here was evidence he'd been punished for his misdeeds.

I felt a flicker of fear—Nadine was alone in the privy—then reminded myself we were hundreds of miles from danger.

He turned the mirror to get another angle, and our eyes met in the reflection. I closed the door and went out the back. I counted to one hundred, and by the time I came around the house he was on the porch wearing a long-sleeved shirt and a huge straw hat with outlines of dolphins and starfish stitched on its crown.

Nadine skipped up beside me before I could say anything to him.

"We're going swimming," she told him.

Sammy gazed at her legs. "I burn easy."

"That wasn't an invitation," she said, then sprinted toward the water.

I watched him watching her and snapped my fingers to get his attention. He didn't look my way when he put a cigarette between his lips and slowly pulled the hat down over his face and the unlit Lucky.

Nadine had a long head start, but the surf slowed her. I caught up as she reached water deep enough to start swimming. The bottom sloped almost imperceptibly, and Sammy was a dot in front of a matchbox by the time we made it out far enough that the highest of the lazy waves lifted our feet off the sand. I remembered the expanse of blue below the mouth of Mississippi on the maps I'd rolled and unrolled for Mr. Erickson and felt at once small and then suddenly connected to a part of the world I'd first seen and smelled when steaming toward New Orleans in 1928. The Gulf was calm and bright. Neck-deep in it, we held hands and turned to the horizon.

"Look." Nadine let go of my hand to point. Where the sky met the water there was a tiny imperfection. "Tanker?" she wondered.

A wave filled my mouth with brine. She remembered the headlines: She put her hand into my trunks and asked, "Want to show me your torpedo?"

Sammy yelled something, and only the worried tone of his voice, not his words, carried out to us. He'd come to the edge of the surf. Nadine raised her free hand to wave. Sammy turned back to the cottage.

She pulled her top up into her armpits, and I stared through the clear water at her breasts before she grabbed my wrists and guided my hands. We bobbed with the surf. A startling cold current wrapped around us and made us both gasp, then vanished. The irony of fooling around in view of Sammy wasn't lost on me, but her hand in my shorts was reassurance that she wanted me, not him. A wave broke over our heads, and for a moment the trough between it and the next was deep enough that we stood in water only waist-deep, the sun gleaming off Nadine's chest and belly. We went a few yards farther from shore, and when she wrapped her legs around my waist, I slid inside her with the sea.

A few hours later Nadine and I were sunbathing and Sammy was reading a year-old copy of *Look* he'd found in an outhouse when from the dunes came the growling of a car with no muffler. Nadine sat up. Her eyes were hidden behind her dark glasses. She looked like a movie star.

"Esther," she said.

A bright red Ford too new to make such a racket topped the last dune going faster than the shell road should have allowed. The coupe slid to a stop, opera blaring from its windows.

The driver's door flew open, and a woman tumbled from the car. "*Bon jour, bébé!*" she yelled over the music. She struggled to her feet and staggered across the sand in heels and a tight skirt. She looked so much like Nadine that I reached out and touched my wife. On the little porch Sammy was looking from one to the other, mouth moving so that it appeared he was trying to sing along with the opera.

Nadine shook her head. "Your shoes are slowing you down, Essie."

"*Oui*, Deenie, but they're *crocodile*." She kicked them off and picked them up, pouring sand from them as she came closer. "Which is the husband?"

I raised my hand.

"You look somehow different, Bobby," she said. "Haircut?"

The music stopped. We three turned to see Sammy standing beside the car. "Loud," he explained. "Turned it off."

"Bobby's dead," Nadine said. "As you know."

"It was a bad joke," Esther admitted. "I try too hard to be the funny sister. Nadine gets to be the pretty sister, so I want to be the funny one."

"But you always end up the mean one instead," Nadine said.

Esther sighed dramatically. "True, Essie's the mean one. Will you forgive me, pretty one?"

Sammy made his way over from the car. "Y'all favor kin," he said.

Esther had a bottle of gin and a jar of olives, and she demanded we join her in drinking martinis. "Imagine vermouth," she suggested. There were no glasses in the cottage, so we drank from jam jars. We four sat on the edge of the porch, boy-girl-boy-girl—Sammy, Esther, me, Nadine—dangling our legs over the sand.

Sammy smacked his lips. "I like gin," he announced.

"Like drinking a Christmas tree," Esther said. "Festive."

Sammy laughed. Nadine was looking out at the Gulf and taking quick sips from her martini. She was far ahead of me, and I gulped to catch up.

"I like your hat," Esther told Sammy, and Nadine snorted. He was wearing the straw thing that was surely Esther's.

He reddened. "I burn easy."

"So," I said, "when was the last time you two girls saw each other?"

Nadine and Esther tipped their drinks, and I waited for one of them to finish and answer. Nadine banged down her empty glass first. "We've made different choices about how to live our lives."

Esther snorted just as Nadine had done a moment before. "One of us lives like the pretty sister," she said, "and one like the mean sister."

"I don't get the joke," Sammy said.

"Nobody made a joke, Sam," Esther told him. "Essie's the *mean* sister, not the funny sister. And it's no joke that the pretty sister likes pretty, pretty boys more than she values her own brains. Did you ever meet dear dead pretty Bobby?"

Without a word Nadine hopped from the porch, and I followed her down to the water. The horizon she studied was made uneven by the ever-present convoy of ships. She sniffed and wiped her nose with the back of her hand.

"That wasn't nice, what she said," I told her.

Behind us the chirp of Esther's voice was followed by the mumble of Sammy's laughter. Nadine reached behind her neck and unclasped the chain on which hung the locket with smiling Bobby inside. Her throw was sidearm but not girlish, and the silver heart skipped off the top of a wave, then hit the face of another and disappeared.

We woke to Esther noisily rooting through our things. She'd slept in the living room after Nadine dismissed with a snort her sister's suggestion that the girls share the bed and the boys make the best of the couch and the kitchen floor (she didn't have keys to any of the other cottages). Sammy, always the gentleman, spent the night on Poppa Dom's backseat.

"You brought two bathing suits but not a single decent dress to wear to church?"

Nadine covered her face with a pillow and hissed.

Esther dumped the suitcase onto the floor and sorted our clothes with her foot. "Walter," she sighed, "please don't tell me you didn't pack a tie."

"Double negative," Nadine said from beneath the pillow.

"No," Esther said, "it's not. 'Didn't never' is a double negative." She kicked my underwear across the floor. "I'm disappointed in you, Nadine."

"Tell her I'm not surprised," Nadine mumbled.

Sammy appeared in the doorway, his cheeks nicked and his ears plugged with shaving lather. "I thought we were in a hurry," he said.

The church was down a dirt track called Egg and Butter Road, and I longed for breakfast when I read the faded sign. I wore a wash jacket Esther had found in the truck of Dom Zanca's Plymouth. It smelled of whiskey and mildew and gasoline, and its sleeves barely covered my elbows. Nadine slumped in her seat while her sister drove the Ford down the soft roads so fast that the noise of sand and pebbles kicked up into the wheel wells took away any possibility of conversation.

Esther had pulled Nadine from bed and made her put on a dress she knew would not fit then gloated, "And to think I used to be the *fat* sister." I almost told Esther that Nadine was pregnant, not pudgy, but I figured if Nadine didn't tell her, she didn't want her sister to know.

The church was taller than it was wide or deep, like a steeple without a sanctuary. It was painted dark brown, its Gothic windows glazed with clear glass.

Esther stamped on the brakes, and the Ford skidded across the sand. "This is the Catholic church?" I hollered over the racket of the busted muffler.

Esther turned off the engine. "No, Episcopal. You're Catholic?"

"Nadine's Catholic."

"No, she's *not*," Esther said. "Bobby is—I'm sorry, Bobby *was*—but she was raised an Episcopalian. She didn't tell you that?"

She hadn't, but I knew this wasn't the time to be anything but supportive of my wife. "Your sister was married in the Catholic Church; she goes to mass. Maybe she used to be an Episcopalian, but she's a Catholic now."

Nadine took my hand and squeezed. Above us the bell rang sharply as a dinner gong.

It was the first time I'd been inside a church in America, the first time I'd been to a church service since Moser told my mother that my father was dead and she began to act as if God was dead as well. There were only two other congregants, an old woman dressed for the kind of winter Florida never witnesses and a man, presumably her son, who wore a lurid purple zoot suit. They sat in the first pew, and Nadine and Sammy and I sat in the last, three empty rows between. Esther played the piano, the church too small for an organ. The upright was as out of tune as the bell, and after she banged out a hymn, Sammy leaned over and whispered, "I once heard that ditty in a whorehouse." Nadine giggled into her hands.

Windblown sand had scratched the window glass, and the view was foggy. Through the panes the clouds looked like they had been penciled onto the sky and erased. The priest's hair was the same smudged gray. He stood in the pulpit and began to read.

"Let mutual love continue. Do not neglect to show hospitality to strangers, for by doing that some have entertained angels without knowing it. Remember those who are in prison, as though you were in prison with them; those who are being tortured, as though you yourselves are being tortured. Let marriage be held in honor by all, and let the marriage bed be kept undefiled; for God will judge fornicators and adulterers. Keep your lives free from the love of money, and be content with what you have; for he has said, 'I will never leave you or forsake you.' So we can say with confidence, 'The Lord is my helper; I will not be afraid. What can anyone do to me?' Remember your leaders, those who spoke the word of God to you; consider the outcome of their way of life, and imitate their faith. Jesus Christ is the same yesterday as today and forever."

I swallowed. It was not the first time the Bible had spoken to me, but it was the most directly I'd ever felt addressed. I looked over at Nadine and found her trying to stare down Esther while Esther fought not to blink, the two of them returned to childhood. Sammy's chin rested on his chest. I was the only one paying attention.

The priest, after appearing to read over silently what he had read aloud, looked up and sniffed. "Word of the Lord."

"Thanks be to God," the zoot-suiter and his mother answered. Esther blinked, Nadine grinned, Sammy woke. My head filled with noise, as if suddenly the fillings in my teeth were picking up radio broadcasts, or the horns Nadine had given me were functioning as antennas. I heard, one atop another, the long honk of a saxophone, an hysterical weather report out of Havana—*huracán!*—and the voice of an announcer describing the chaos of a World Series game's bottom of the eleventh with unnatural calm: *Bases loaded . . . two outs . . . full count.* No one's mouth moved, but I heard Nadine's mocking *unbelievable* mixed with Sammy asking "What's the good word?" and the jingle of the pennies and dimes in the pockets of his pants when he hurriedly pulled them up.

The din was so intense I couldn't make out the rest of what the priest said. As I walked up the aisle toward the altar, the dots and dashes of Morse code that'd haunted me returned so loudly that I was amazed the racket wasn't leaking from my ears.

I knelt, and when the Bread of Heaven was stuck to my tongue, it was like the power had gone out. The world was quiet. I heard Sammy slurp wine, the *shush* of the priest's robes, the snap of a wafer made two. Back in the pew, listening to Esther slam out another hymn, I tried to hold the Body there forever, but slowly it dissolved, and all that was left was the sour-sweet hint of the Blood—and then the dots and dashes were back, albeit more faintly.

The rain began as we drove home, another good reason not to talk. In the cottage Nadine and I went into the bedroom, shed our humiliating clothes, and climbed into bed. She went to sleep while I observed a small water stain growing incrementally on the ceiling above us and listened to Sammy and Esther playing hearts in the kitchen, the Morse code inside my head fading until the rain on the roof was louder. I thought about the priest's advice. Nadine snored, Sammy cursed when he lost a hand, and instead of thinking about POWs, the shoebox of money, and Nadine and Sammy abed, I thought about Esther taunting my wife.

The girls who'd done the sensible thing were no better off than the wild girls. For years the war had deprived them of cookies and steaks and car trips to Biloxi. There hadn't been Mardi Gras parades since 1941. In the name of stability the sensible girls had married dull boys with futures when they could've had their pick of poor guys who liked to dance, and now their sacrifices didn't matter. Sensible or wild, the war took their brothers, their fathers, their fun boyfriends, their boring husbands. Nadine had been the brave sister when she married Bobby. I closed my eyes and listened to the leaks pinging into the pans set out to catch them.

Near midday we woke and put on our bathing suits and ran through the storm to the outhouses. I didn't want to let Nadine out of my sight even for the moment it took her to relieve herself, so I made a joke of sticking my foot in the door and pretending to sell her Fuller Brushes. She laughed and laughed.

When we got back to the cottage, Esther's red Ford was gone, along with Esther and Sammy. They didn't leave a note. On the kitchen table two hands had been dealt and left facedown. I pulled out a chair for Nadine, she sat, I took the chair opposite, and we played hearts while outside the gray rainy midday became a gray rainy afternoon, then we switched to gin rummy as the gray rainy afternoon faded into a gray rainy evening. We drank cold coffee from breakfast, ate a make-do dinner of leftovers, stiff bacon and cold toast.

When the wind rattled the door, it sounded like a fist knocking, but after the first time I was fooled and opened it and got soaked, I threw the flimsy bolt and we ignored the storm.

"I'll bet they went to the college," Nadine said, breaking what might've been an hour of silence. I thought she sounded slightly jealous, but I hoped I was wrong. "Gin," she said.

I looked at the fan of cards she laid down. "The college?"

"Esther's a teacher at the normal school." She tallied points on the back of a matchbook. "French and English composition and *music*—can you believe it after hearing her play the piano?" Her voice was stretched thin by false nonchalance.

Nadine shuffled and began to deal. "My parents were both librarians, and I was going to be one too," she blurted. "I loved books—I *love* books: novels, poetry." Cards piled up in front of us both, and she kept dealing. I'd never seen her read anything except *Life* and the newspaper. "But I met Bobby at Pontchartrain Beach and—"

She looked down when she ran out of cards. The entire deck was spread between us.

"I feel bad I didn't know you wanted to be a librarian," I said. "I feel bad I didn't know you love books."

She leaned across the table and put her hands on top of mine. "I feel bad I never told you."

Wind shook the door, thunder stomped the porch floor.

Nadine looked like she was going to cry. "I think that's them, not the storm."

◆◆◆

We spent the next morning under a Florida sky so blasted by sunlight that it looked like a dome of polished silver. The Gulf was calm and flat, the ships on the horizon constant as a line of distant islands. Sammy dressed in long sleeves, his one pair of pants, and mismatched socks, masked himself with a towel, and lay down on the sand. Esther wore a green sundress and the hat she'd reclaimed from Sammy and sat beside him in a canvas folding chair with a book, a cigarette, and a ten-o'clock jam-jar martini.

Nadine and I built a sandcastle. She wore one of my work shirts loose over her swimsuit, and at first I wondered why, then remembered the way Esther had sniggered while Nadine struggled with the zipper of the dress her sister demanded she wear to church.

After a long silence during which I dug a moat and grew drowsy in the sun, Esther threw an olive at Sammy, and it bounced off his thigh. "You ninety-seven-pound weakling," she said.

"I'm sick and tired of being a scarecrow," he answered from behind his towel. I was surprised to hear his voice; I'd been sure he was asleep. He unwrapped his head to see what'd hit him, picked up the olive and blew off the sand, and popped it into his mouth. "Charles Atlas says he can give me a *real* body. I'll gamble a stamp and get his *free* book!" He put a hand to each temple and squeezed until his tongue popped out. "Dynamic tension!" he yelled.

"I want to swim," Nadine announced.

I followed her into the water, watching the tails of my drab work shirt darken, then stick to her backside, then float. Nadine was up to her armpits when she tipped her head back and said, "Catch me." I reached for her, and for a moment she was gone; then her toes broke the surface five feet in front of me, and I held her shoulders while she floated on her back, eyes closed. She fanned her arms and legs like I used to do as a child when making an angel in the snow. I kissed her upside-down mouth. Esther screamed laughter, and Nadine opened her eyes. "Once she took a red pencil to a love letter Bobby sent me, corrected his spelling and grammar, sent it back to him. He thought I did it, thought I'd given him a D-minus."

There was a commotion from the beach. Nadine wiggled out of my grip and stood on the bottom, and when I turned, there was Sammy, clad only in his underwear, high-stepping into the water, heading toward us. Behind him Esther was pulling her dress over her head.

"Oh, for God's sake," Nadine said.

The first short wave that splashed her made Esther's slip nearly transparent. Beneath it she did not appear to be wearing a brassiere or panties. Sammy dove into the Gulf when he was knee-deep and came up laughing and choking on salt water and holding his shorts with both hands to keep them on. His bruises had faded to pale yellows and greens. He checked over his shoulder to see where Esther was, and when he caught sight of her—a pinup girl under flimsy lingerie—he shook his head to clear his vision.

"Essie!" Nadine hollered, her voice like a chiding mother's.

"Deenie!" her sister joyfully yelled back, and waved. She pulled off her slip, balled it up, and tossed it at Sammy. Her nipples were darker than Nadine's, and I felt loutish for noticing. Esther stood naked and grinning in the brilliant sunlight, waves covering and uncovering her like pale blue veils. Sammy looked my way, his face blank with surprise.

Nadine took off the shirt she'd worn over her bathing suit and swung it by one arm. Esther laughed while Nadine tugged off her swimsuit's top. Sammy covered his eyes with his hands, uncovered them to catch his falling shorts, then used one hand to hold up his pants and one to hide the fact he was peeking.

Esther threw her head back and hooted when Nadine pushed the bottom of her suit down over her knees and tripped out of it. They fought through the water to each other, and I wondered if they were going to slap or hug. When they stood close, Nadine said something, Esther's eyes dropped to her sister's stomach and her smile went flat, then came back twice as large. Esther fell to her knees, a wave submerging her head, and when the trough revealed her, she had her ear pressed to Nadine's bellybutton.

They held hands and walked toward the beach. Hair wet and flat against their heads and necks, they were twin Oceanids. I couldn't hear what they said, but it looked like apology and forgiveness.

Sammy and I trailed them into shallow water. "We don't deserve to witness such beauty," I said, and cringed to think how similar this response was to the response when I'd found Nadine and Sammy abed. "At least you don't," I added. Sammy hung his head and made a noise in his throat.

It was piss-poor repentance, especially given the erection that held up his boxers. He followed me to the beach, collected his clothes, and went around the corner of the last cottage.

There were a few fingers of Esther's martini left in the jar stuck in the sand. I drank them in one long swallow. She fancied good gin. Her novel was French, thin, and as best as I could tell, both pornographic and surrealist. I puzzled out half a page, my twenty-years-stale schoolboy's skills no match for Dadaist fornication, and gave up. Sammy sat on the little porch of the cottage he'd dressed behind and pretended he wasn't watching me.

I found Esther and Nadine in the front room, both in calico sundresses I hadn't seen before. Esther was combing Nadine's hair. They were red-nosed from the sun, puffy around the eyes from crying, and grinning and blushing like sheepish, guilty girls.

"I should know better," Esther said.

Nadine nodded. "Me too."

I was still stunned by the sight of my wife and my sister-in-law naked and sparkling. What could I do but blush and grin along with them? "You two are wild," I said.

They beamed. "After lunch," Esther said, "let's take parts in a play, one with lots of kissing."

We did not, thank goodness, act out a play with lots of kissing, but Sammy came to lunch when Esther called him, and we sat at table and ate baked beans and toast, then played bridge on the porch, the sisters giddy and chatty and untroubled by our manly gloom.

After a few hands Sammy got up without excusing himself and walked down toward the water. "Don't wait up," Esther joked, and followed him across the sand. They sat down where they had earlier, and Esther again read to him from her French novelette.

"Do you think she's translating?" Nadine jeered.

I bit my lip and wished she didn't care what Sammy was up to. "Let's start over," I said.

Nadine cocked her head. "Start over?"

"Let's forget everything—Bobby, the day I came home and found you with Sammy, when we were fat and why we were fat. Let's start now, right now." I slapped the porch floor.

"Now," she agreed. "Right now."

Nadine packed a picnic, and I followed her down to the Gulf's edge. We stood back to back like duelists, the top of Nadine's head bumping between my shoulders.

"Go," she said, and we headed down the beach the hundred paces we'd agreed upon, turned, and pretended it was the first time we'd ever seen each other. She waved. I retraced my hundred steps, and she retraced hers.

"Nadine Keneally," she said.

"Walter Schmidt."

"Charmed."

We walked along the beach telling each other things we hadn't told each other when we first met. Nadine began her story before she was born. Her father was a young librarian at Tulane, her mother a student at Newcomb. They met when her mother tried to return a waterlogged volume of Hopkins she'd dropped in the bath. Nadine grew up in a house made of books: tables leveled with scientific monographs, puppies penned inside piles of encyclopedias. She took clarinet and piano and ballet lessons. In college she was an English major.

"But I liked chemistry better," she admitted. "I wanted to be like Marie Curie." Then she met Bobby, "who was no Pierre." When I looked confused, Nadine explained, "Marie's husband. She shared the first Nobel with him and another chemist, then got her own."

Bobby went to the Pacific and was killed, Nadine began to eat and eat and go to movies, and Sammy sat down with her at the soda fountain and called me over. Each detail she provided made me love her more. "You know the rest," she said. "Or am I supposed to invent something to fill the time between then and now?"

"Let's not lie," I said.

We went into the dunes and spread a thin blanket.

I told my life backwards, beginning on the day her story ended, ending the day I came to New Orleans. She clicked her tongue when I told her about Mrs. Erickson, laughed when I told her I'd known nothing about baseball and so thought Ruth was a woman. I told her how the sweetness of New Orleans's air surprised me, how during my first August I'd turned on the cold tap and held my hand under it, waiting for the water to cool before I realized lukewarm was as cool as I could have in Louisiana in the summertime.

"But what about before that?" she wanted to know.

I told her about my mother dying. She reached out and touched me—our first touch. I couldn't tell her about Ilse, or about the lie I'd told Andreas, even if we were starting anew. I decided it wasn't lying to leave an empty space—she hadn't been lying when she didn't describe every moment of her life—and I told her about the pictures of my father—my only memories of him—and about the game of knock-the-man-down Andreas and I used to play in the street when we were boys.

Nadine leaned into the kiss I bent to give her. For the first time we saw in each other more than what had been taken from us or we'd stupidly thrown away.

When the kiss ended, I asked her to marry me.

Esther was thrilled and Sammy stopped sulking when we came back and Nadine told them we were getting married. "But you're already married," Sammy said, then narrowed his eyes. "You are, aren't you?"

"You were there," I reminded him. "You signed the license."

Sammy kept squinting.

Esther decided our playacting wasn't dramatic enough, so we headed for Egg and Butter Road. The priest was napping in a pew when we arrived, and sleepy enough he appeared not to notice when, standing in front of him, we took off our wedding rings to put them back on. He held the prayer book but recited the verses with his eyes closed. He opened them to tell us we were man and wife and to see how much his tip was—five dollars, from Esther.

"Don't spend it all in one place, Padre," she said.

We went to an oyster house and ate until we were stuffed, diets be damned, and then drank watery beers and listened to the jukebox play scratched and hissing blues records. Nadine and I slow-danced to every song, no matter the music's speed, while Sammy and Esther sat watching. Finally they joined us on the creaking dance floor, Sammy's light feet impressing everyone. The zoot-suiter from the church came in and used what I was convinced was Esther's fiver for beers and pennies for the illegal slot machine.

"Hey, Jim, I know you, daddy-daddy," he said as he passed me.

On our second wedding night we played at being bashful and fumbling. After Nadine fell asleep, I pulled back the sheet to look at the slope of her belly. I thought about Sammy's gift to us the first time we wed: a pair of salt and pepper shakers for Nadine's collection, a bride and a groom in white dress and tuxedo. At their feet, the word *Before*. When the shakers were turned around, the groom wore overalls and a beard shadow and the bride's belly was round as a ball under her polka-dotted housecoat. *After,* that side said.

◆◆◆

For three days I pretended I was nothing more than a honeymooner from New Orleans on a beach in Florida with my bride, my best friend, and my new sister-in-law. I didn't think about the many mistakes I'd made, the innumerable hurts I'd suffered and caused. I was American to my marrow: happy, silly, optimistic. Esther kept her clothes on. Sammy sat at her feet dutifully listening to her read French, smiling; his brow wrinkled while he waited, like a dog, to hear his name or a random word he understood.

"I think they make a good couple," Nadine proclaimed, and she seemed earnestly approving.

Nadine and I frolicked in the Gulf, the Ford's cramped backseat, the dunes. We giggled and shushed each other when in the middle of the night we made the bedsprings sing. Pouring breakfast coffee Esther shook her head and clicked her tongue.

"You are, my dears, perhaps overacting your parts—Walter, she's already with child, remember?"

Sammy, who spent his nights alone in the Plymouth, cleared his throat and flipped a pancake.

Undaunted by her sister's bad review, Nadine and I stuck to the script, happy to play stock newlyweds. I slept more soundly than I had since my father went off to fight. My dreams were so colorful and complex that in the morning I could never remember more than a single weird moment: The shells of an open oyster became a butterfly's flapping wings, a furry black poodle puppy grew the extra legs of a tarantula. I woke dazzled by dreams to find Nadine beside me, my dazzling new bride, her belly growing toward the salt shaker's prophesied *After*.

Very early Friday morning I was awakened by a dream in which flowering trees grew from my shoes. Nadine snored softly, and when I couldn't fall back to sleep, I eased out of bed. Only sand came from my brogans when I shook them, but the memory of branches and white and pink dogwood blossoms kept me barefoot. Esther and Sammy were asleep on the couch, both naked at least to the waist, a blanket modestly covering the rest of them, and I tiptoed past.

I walked along the beach. In the gray early light the pelicans cruising over the waves in small squadrons were the color of dust. Out where sky met water, there was an orange pop like a match head igniting. I watched a smudge of smoke dirty the brightening sky and knew without doubt I'd just seen a U-boat torpedo a tanker.

I looked down at my feet and saw a flash. Nadine's locket had been washed up by the same wave that had at some point gently rocked the ship now aflame; inside the locket Bobby was grinning, grinning, grinning. I scooped up a handful of sand, sifted it through my fingers, and found not the locket but an ingot of sea glass, a shard of a milk bottle or a pickle jar polished into a perfect circle. When I looked back to the horizon, the ship still burned. I headed back to the honeymoon cottage.

From the top of the porch's steps, through the screen door, I saw Sammy and Esther on the couch, naked in each other's arms, blanket kicked to the floor. I realized I was looking at a version of the scene I'd witnessed not two weeks earlier, though this time Sammy was in bed with my sister-in-law, not my wife, so why now was I filled with cuckold's rage? Why now did I feel the urge to kill him? Why now did I lurch toward the son of a bitch, ready to choke him to death?

Sammy and Esther sat up when I slammed open the screen door, but my fury evaporated when Esther grabbed for the blanket to cover herself and Sammy stood quickly to shield her from me.

"Where'd you come from?" he asked.

Esther's face was bright red, but she laughed. "What are *you* blushing about?"

I turned to the mirror and saw my face was redder than hers. I looked at Sammy. My flush and my shaking hands and my racing heart were caused by betrayal and the burning tanker, by Sammy and a U-boat.

Nadine came into the kitchen rubbing her eyes and smiling, but when she saw Sammy pulling up his boxer shorts and Esther under the blanket, she colored darker than I had. There was a silent moment during which Sammy pretended to sort through the seashells he and Esther had collected the day before.

Esther said, "I'm making coffee."

Sammy stood casually covering his crotch with his hands. "I'll drink some," he said, and then shrugged. He hooked his thumb at the door. "Pretty sunrise?" he asked me.

I thought of the burning tanker and swallowed. Nadine seemed unable to decide where to stand. She shuffled from the kitchen to the living room and then back to the kitchen.

Coffee burbled in the percolator. "We're out of cream," Esther apologized.

"Then we *must* go and get some," I said, and all three of them bobbed their heads excitedly, happy to have the errand's distraction.

We took the ear-splitting Ford, Sammy behind the wheel, boys in front, girls in back, and headed for the general store that was also the post office and the police station. Sammy tuned the radio through inch after inch of static, whistling as if he'd found a clear station and was joining in on a tune. I wondered if he was feeling, at long last, guilty for what he'd done—and then I wondered if he'd staged the scene with hopes that I would wander in and find him with Esther, if he'd wanted to rub it in, wanted to prove to me he could have any woman he wanted—my wife, her sister—and then I wondered if the person he'd really wanted to see him naked in bed with Esther was Nadine. We passed Egg and Butter Road while I considered the possibilities. Maybe it was Esther's idea?

The rusted black-and-white sheriff's Dodge was parked beside the gas pump, and the deputy leaning against it was none other than the Episcopalian zoot-suiter. He wore a drab uniform and knuckled a bebop beat on the fender while he watched Nadine and Esther climb the porch steps. A wisp of smoke rose from behind the store, the torpedoed tanker burning on a horizon we were now too far inland to see. If I hadn't witnessed the far-off explosion, I wouldn't have noticed the gray thread that from where I stood could've been coming from the store's chimney pipe. The sheriff and the postmaster were at the porch rail. The lawman was handsome as a movie star, the postmaster homely as a Hollywood sidekick. They touched the brims of their hats when the women passed.

The store was dim and smelled of apples and cheese and sardines. I went to the Coca-Cola cooler and found a pint of cream amid the soda pop. While Sammy walked up and down the four narrow isles, I took two Nehis out to Nadine and Esther.

"Get some beer," Sammy suggested when I returned.

The postmaster came in so we could pay him. Nadine and Esther were sipping their orange sodas out on the porch with the good-looking sheriff.

"Miss Esther told me to give you her mail and have you buy crackers," the postmaster said to Sammy, passing him a single envelope and a tin of saltines.

"You have a telephone?" Sammy asked. "I need to make a call."

The postmaster took from a hook behind the counter a skeleton key tied to a foot-long tin fob that was painted white and covered with city names and numbers.

"Where to?"

"New Orleans."

"Who're you going to call?" I asked.

"Time and temperature," Sammy said, then winked at me.

"Don't do that again," I told him.

The postmaster searched the list on the fob and told Sammy, "Six bits if you keep it short, dollar if you don't."

Sammy shrugged. "All right."

The postmaster licked his pencil and added the number to the receipt he was making out.

"Miss Esther have an account?" Sammy said.

"Yessir, she does."

"Put that all on it, then," Sammy told him. "And a Coke." He pulled a little bottle from the cooler, popped its top, and drank it in one long swallow. "Two Cokes," he said, and opened another.

I remembered the Coca-Cola I'd once poured in the gutter while following Sammy's diet rules and grabbed two little bottles for myself. "I'll pay for these," I said, slapping down a dime.

"Want them urnge sodies on her bill?" the postmaster asked me, pointing out the window at Nadine and Esther.

"Yep," Sammy said.

The postmaster led us into the back room and used the skeleton key to open an antique padlock on a wooden box mounted on the wall. Inside was the telephone. He had Sammy tell him the number, which he wrote down and then read to the operator. He handed Sammy the receiver and stood with his arms crossed, watching Sammy wait for whomever he was calling to answer. I went back into the store to give them some privacy.

Nadine and Esther were talking on the porch, their voices so alike I couldn't tell who was speaking. Days-old copies of the Mobile and New Orleans newspapers were on the floor beside the shelf that held fishhooks and bobbers; they were creased and crumpled as if they'd been used to wrap something. I smoothed a few and read the headlines from the days I'd managed to avoid by sunbathing and swimming. Communist partisans had killed Mussolini. In Leipzig a munitions manufacturer had staged a lavish banquet, then blown up the table, killing himself and the hundred guests who smoked cigars and sipped old cognac. Newspaper correspondents who'd gotten ahead of the advancing troops were liberating concentration camps, and captured SS guards were being made to dig mass graves and bury their victims. In Tuscany the Nazis annihilated the entire male population of a town. War crimes and Rionado Rum shared the page with guaranteed watch repairs and reports of twelve-year-olds armed with bazookas fighting last stands in Berlin.

I went onto the porch, and Nadine handed me her Nehi, then leaned over the rail and threw up.

"Momma's sick," Sammy said. We all turned. He stood in the doorway wringing his hands. "Got to get back to New Orleans—Daddy's at the end of his rope, stupid old man."

"Momma?" I asked. "Daddy?" It was the first mention of his family I'd ever heard.

"Not all of us are lucky enough to be orphans," he snapped.

Esther sighed. "We're all too old to be orphans, Sam."

"Never too old," the sheriff said. Esther snorted.

We drove back to the cottage and packed. I didn't want to leave. More than I feared Stewart, I feared the playacting would end as soon as we drove off. Nadine and I would return to the roles we played before: disappointed widow, untrustworthy immigrant. Sammy stuffed his bag like the house was on fire, threw it out the open front door, and went down on his knees before Esther. "Come with me."

"Come with you?" She looked terrified.

"Come with me."

"Sam," she said, "you know I can't. I have a job, this house. Take care of your mother and your father and come back."

"Go fuck your sheriff," Sammy said, then began to get up.

Esther slapped him as he rose. "You're an asshole." Her voice was flat and angry. "I knew it the day I met you, but I hoped I'd misjudged. I didn't, you asshole."

"Come on, Walter." Sammy rubbed his cheek and looked at the floor. "Let's go, Nadine." He stomped out.

I picked up our suitcase.

"Warm up the car," Nadine told me. She sounded upset.

In the Plymouth's backseat Sammy sat looking straight ahead. The engine was already running. "Bitch," he whispered when I got behind the wheel.

"She invited you to come back. You're the one who was nasty."

"Bitch," he insisted.

Nadine came down the steps and across the sand. Esther stood at the rail, her arms crossed over her chest. "Take care of her, Walter. Deenie's the good sister," she called while Nadine got in.

"Bitch," Sammy muttered.

"Shut up," Nadine told him. "She's too good for you, and you're too stupid and mean and selfish to ever deserve anyone as good as she is—so shut up, shut up, *shut up.*"

When I looked into the rearview, Sammy pulled closed an invisible zipper across his pursed lips.

Daylight made the road new. The jungle now on my right was threadbare, the Gulf on my left edged by a dirty rind of sand, and many of the filling stations and BEER FISH WHISKEY roadhouses were boarded up. *Thanks a Lot, Hitler!* was painted across the soaped windows of one.

Sammy snored, obviously faking, and Nadine studied one of the newspapers I'd skimmed at the store—I recognized its headlines. She read intently while I did my best to keep my eyes on the road. I feared the *Times-Picayune* was slandering me. *Thanks a lot, Hitler,* I thought. The honeymoon was truly over. It was time to return to life as it had been.

"What's so interesting?" I asked when I could no longer stand the silence.

Nadine looked up and blinked into focus the world out the window. "I want to move." On her lap the paper was open to the classifieds. "There's a cute double on Dufossat." She tapped the little picture. "We could rent out half. I don't want starting over to be over."

I nearly drove into the ditch when I leaned to kiss her. Sammy's fake snoring stopped, but his lips stayed zipped while Nadine and I swapped plans for gardens and a teeter-totter for the baby, a fig tree in the side yard, the advertised job selling siding that seemed to her something I would be good at. I loved her for the kindness of saying, "How about life insurance? You could sell that."

We playfully bickered over baby names and crossed into Alabama. Behind me I could feel Sammy stretched out across the seat, watching the blue sky that filled the Plymouth's back window, burning with jealousy.

Sammy had me drop him off on the corner of Elysian Fields and Abundance. It was one of a run of street names I'd always liked when I passed them on the bus to Pontchartrain Beach—Pleasure, Humanity, Benefit, Treasure, Abundance, Agriculture, Industry. It was late, the streetlights toning the night sepia. Nadine was asleep with her head in my lap. Sammy saw her there when he ducked into the driver's window to tell me something, and I watched his face twist and untwist and wished I could feel bad for the silent gloating I'd been doing since she nodded off in Mississippi.

"Your parents live around here?" I asked.

"Don't tell nobody where I am."

"You're my friend; don't worry."

He flinched, then picked up his bag and walked away.

Nadine slept through the city, and I carried her into the house and put her to bed and went to sleep beside her hopeful she and I could keep alive the new life we'd started on the beach. Her belly was growing rounder; I was sure I could see a change, the baby inside her now a dozen weeks old, and the simple fact that her body was different hinted that starting anew could work.

The last prayer I'd offered was a wish that my father not only come home from the war but that he come home with bread that night, and when he didn't, I'd given up on prayers, but something had happened to me in that weird little church in Florida, something that made me say a quick prayer, noting Sammy's plight as if there was nothing I could do about his troubles beyond praying for him.

The paperboy mistakenly tossed the Saturday morning news onto my porch, so I didn't have to steal Poppa Dom's. Hitler was dead, a suicide, the Reds claimed. Berlin had fallen, Munich had fallen. I read twice the news of the city in which I'd been born, the city my father had left to fight Americans and never returned to, the city in which my mother had died and where she lay buried, the city in which I'd grown from baby to orphan to jerk. Each time I read the news I felt nothing but happiness that my enemy had been defeated.

Below the fold was the report that Truman had banned V-E revelry. We were to keep working, keep using our ration books for twelve more months. I knew my neighbors would grumble, but it was for me as exciting as the news of Hitler's death. The war, as far as Truman was concerned, was good as over, and he, like me, was planning for the peaceful years to come, the prosperity ahead.

As for the *Times-Picayune*, the war was over by page 2. The next few pages were filled with no fewer than three reports of the strawberry harvest in north Louisiana (lack of railcars, pie-eating contest in Pineville, low prices caused by surplus). Holmes ran page after page of ads for summer clothes for men, women, and children. In place of doomsday predictions about the rising river were humorous notes about what the almost-flood left behind: a dozen mannequins in fancy dress that had first looked like a family of rich drowning victims, a disoriented but healthy milk cow with a brand that seemed to prove she'd somehow survived the trip downriver from Missouri to Mississippi. There was no mention of the tanker I'd seen torpedoed.

The sports section was long as a Russian novel. I checked the classifieds to see if the double on Dufossat was still advertised and was pleased to see its price cut from $9,000 to $8,500. Three olive-drab seaplanes flew upriver, buzzing like houseflies. I took a long breath. It was time to start anew.

My plan was to use 728 Milan as collateral for a loan, and then to rent and use the income from it and from half the double on Dufossat to pay the mortgage on both halves. G.I.s would be home from Europe and looking for nice little places in which to start families, and I'd have two to offer. Soon I'd be rid of the assorted Zancas and Bobby's ghost.

I'd parked Poppa Dom's Plymouth in front of his house and put the keys in his mailbox, so we took the streetcar up Magazine. It was kitten season Uptown. Rascal's square-headed bastards were everywhere on Milan, and eleven blocks away on Dufossat a half-dozen of some other tom's striped offspring were basking in the sun on the front porch of 1030 and 1032. They scattered when the man selling the house opened the gate.

"Cats come free," he joked as he fought the front door's lock.

The man who'd sold 728 Milan to me had seemed uninterested in my money, but Jim Riley was so nervous you would've thought he'd forged the deed. "Polished floors!" he cheered. "New toilet!" he hollered. He seemed surprised to find indoor plumbing. He stepped into the bathtub and yelled, "Would you look at this!" In the kitchen he stood before the stove with his mouth open in sham wonder. "Think of the soup," he murmured, and Nadine laughed. He grinned uncomfortably, and it took me a second to realize his tic was supposed to be a wink. I winked back, and he quit twitching.

The left side of the double mirrored the right: A side hall from a sunny front parlor led past three small bedrooms and the bathroom and ended at the swinging kitchen door. Jim Riley repeated his shouting about the floors, toilet, and tub. Only in the second kitchen did he say something new.

"Property line's right down the middle, so you're getting a good solid home, half you can rent to help make the note, and two deep lots, all for nine thousand dollars."

"It says eight thousand five hundred in the paper," Nadine said, unfolding a swatch of classifieds. Jim Riley's lips moved when he read.

"Give you eight," I bargained.

Riley's tic was no longer an attempt at winking. "$8,250," he bid.

Nadine held out her hand. "I want the key *now.*"

"No one's getting dinner out of this," Riley said cryptically as he took a pair of keys off his ring and handed them to her. He sighed like he'd made a terrible mistake. Nadine wrote a contract on the back of a grocery receipt she found in her purse. Riley looked like he was trying to figure a way to call off the deal, but I knew if he'd dropped the price he needed to sell, even if he wished he could get more. "You owe me $8,250." He pointed to the keys. "You don't get me that by . . . well, next week?"

I nodded, and then he nodded.

"You don't get me the money by *next week*, I get those back."

I owned the place on Milan outright, and I knew there would be no trouble getting a mortgage for a double that guaranteed rental income. I shook his hand, and Riley did his best to smile. "It's a good house," he said.

There was a stationer's shop by the streetcar stop, and in the window I saw books. I led Nadine in and had her pick a few: Walter Scott, Anthony Trollope, *The Moon and Sixpence*. I got myself a two-volume set of Sherlock Holmes stories. The stationer wrapped the books in brown paper, and Nadine happily hugged them all the way home.

On Milan Street she dumped dirty laundry from the suitcase she'd taken to Florida, filled it with her mother's silver and a change

"Andreas?"

He looked to see where the guard was—twenty feet away, drinking from a fountain—and I followed his gaze.

"Andreas?"

He went back to work as if I wasn't there.

"Andreas?" I reached out, and he ducked as if I'd thrown a punch.

"That'll be that," the guard said behind me. He tapped my shoulder with his billy club.

"Andreas?" I asked again.

The club came down harder. "Let him be," the guard said.

"Andreas?"

The POW chopped dirt and wouldn't look up.

"Hey, stupid, do I have to split your skull?" the guard calmly asked as he poked me in the kidney with his billy. "Move along and let him be."

The POW started whistling a tune I swore was the Morse code that'd been haunting me for weeks. My shoes were heavy with mud, and I felt like I was losing my mind—my cousin a POW and secret messages in every song I heard.

"I'm so goddamn tired of the war," I told the guard.

"Who isn't?" he wondered.

In the car I was sure I wasn't mistaken. I turned around and headed for Dufossat.

I hired movers to haul our things to the new house, agreed to pay them double for short notice, Sunday labor, and rush service.

The front parlor was littered with sheets of uncrumpled newspaper, but it looked like Nadine had unwrapped only a few of her salt and pepper shakers. I found her in the middle bedroom, lying beneath the fan with a cloth covering her face. She hugged a mop bucket under one arm.

"You okay?" I asked, but I was thinking about Andreas.

She lifted the washrag from her eyes. "Jim Riley came past *twice,* and both times there was someone in his car with him. I think he'd like to get more than we're going to give him, wouldn't he?"

I sat on the edge of the bed and took her hand. I wondered what she'd do if I confessed to her that my lies had killed Ilse. I forced myself to pay attention, repeated in my head what she had just said.

"I rented out the house on Milan before I could even put up a sign," I told her. "There'll be enough from rent to pay all the bills and have a little left over each month, put that little away, and at the end of the year use that money to buy another place, then another—and then another."

Nadine propped herself up onto her elbow and gagged into the mop bucket. "I can't keep anything down. This is what I get for being so smug about not feeling sick at first."

I wondered if Ilse had been far enough along to get sick. "You want another washcloth?"

"Please," she said. "There're some in the icebox."

It turned out the electricity had been on all along but that Jim Riley had removed all the lightbulbs. The Frigidaire hummed. In it a tin bowl of wet, folded washcloths sat beside a dozen Jax. I opened a bottle and drank it in three swallows. I popped a second and carried it back to the bedroom. "Who brought the beer?" I asked when I put the cloth on her forehead.

"I walked up to the grocery on Prytania for bread and salami and beer. I think I'm sick because I got too hot."

I pressed the bottle against her neck, and she shivered. I kissed the cold patch of skin where her jugular pulsed and hoped she would make love to me so I could think about her body instead of remembering how I had repeated to Andreas what he'd told me Ilse looked like under her clothes.

"Feels good," she said. "But let me rest, Lucky Boy."

The telephone rang, and when I lifted the receiver, a voice demanded, "Why you always hassling me?"

◆◆◆

Nadine poked me awake and said, "Someone's banging on the door." I pulled on a pair of pants while the loud knocking continued. As I came down the hall, I saw in the shade covering the front door's glass the silhouette of a policeman in profile, but when I opened the door what I found was Sammy. He was in full-dress Army Air Corps uniform; the outline of his hat had fooled me. He stuck out his hand like he was after my vote and asked, "What's the good word?"

"Never say that to me again," I told him.

He let his hand drop. "Let's take a drive?" His right eye was swollen shut, and when he coughed and spat, the wad was bloody.

"I'll get a shirt," I said. He tried to step inside; I pushed him back. "I'll get a shirt," I said again, and closed the door.

Nadine was still in bed. "Who was it?" she asked.

"Sammy," I told her. "I'll be right back."

She turned her face into the pillow.

Sammy was behind the wheel of the Plymouth, and when he held out his hand, I didn't think before I dropped the keys into his open palm.

We were on Annunciation when he said, "Stewart beat my ass and then told my daddy he'd kill me if I didn't get him his money."

I looked at his swollen eye and resisted the urge to poke at it to see if it was makeup. I wouldn't have put it past him to chew a few strawberries so he could spit what looked like blood. For a thousand dollars I wouldn't even have put it past him to hire someone to beat him so he could make me feel guilty.

"Told him he'd break my momma's legs."

"Why don't you just walk into a bank dressed like that and take out a loan under the name Captain Asshole?"

He took a swing at me while he kept his eyes on the road, and I grabbed his wrist and twisted until his shoulder popped. "Goddamn!" he yelped. He jerked the wheel and stomped on the brake, and the car came to a sliding stop with the Plymouth's bumper touching the post of a STOP sign. I didn't let go. "What the hell?" he demanded.

"You gave me that money because I caught you in bed with my wife, and now you're trying to make me feel sorry for you?"

"Stewart—"

"Bullshit," I said, and cranked his wrist so hard that he bent forward to escape the pain and banged his head on the steering wheel.

I looked over Sammy's shoulders and neck and saw the curve of a Packard's fender, then witnessed the amazing sight: There at the wheel, pausing to light a cigar at the STOP sign Sammy'd nearly knocked down, was Stewart the bookie.

"Well, well, well," I said. "Sambo, look who's here." I twisted his arm in the other direction, and he sat up. When he saw Stewart, he ducked so violently it's a wonder he didn't dislocate his shoulder. He curled on the floor gasping, and all at once I smelled excrement—he'd shit his pants. It hadn't been an act; he was sure Stewart would kill him. Sammy's terror shocked me. What'd happened to the unflappable blowhard? Stewart shook out his match and looked my way. It appeared he was trying to remember where he'd seen me before. Oddly, I felt no fear. The reek made me squint, and I was more disgusted by Sammy's weakness than afraid. Before Stewart could recognize me, the driver of the car behind his honked her hometown as much as he did, though he might not now know he loved it, that I wanted to be tied to New Orleans like he was, to be unable to leave it like he was. I wanted to belong to someplace; I wanted to live a long boring life; I wanted to apologize for the pain I'd caused.

"All debts paid," I said.

The part of the plan I couldn't tell Sammy was that I wanted to apologize to Andreas, and I'd have to kidnap him to do that. He'd think I was crazy, and maybe I was crazy, but kidnapping Andreas— or whoever he was—would give me the liberty to stay put—and it would give Sammy the same freedom. Why was it impossible for the POW I kept seeing to be my cousin? Why was it impossible that I'd heard him ask me for help? It wasn't impossible—it wasn't. And even if the man wasn't Andreas—and I had to admit he might not be—none of us would be worse off for the adventure. We could snatch him, make our bets, and the worst outcome would be that Sammy would be able to pay off Stewart. Then we'd turn the POW loose. Who would believe him when he professed his innocence—a *German*! A *Nazi*!—and claimed he'd been abducted? From what the newspapers reported, the punishment for escaping for a few hours or a day was being made to do work a little dirtier than they'd been doing when they absconded. So the worst that would happen to this man—if he wasn't Andreas after all—was that he'd have to shovel a taller pile of shit or muck out a nastier drain. And if he was my cousin, I could apologize. He didn't need to be caught to win the bet. I could hide him, teach him English, have him help me fix up houses.

"I don't know," Sammy said again.

None of my tangled motives and history would mean anything to Sammy. He had more immediate needs—money to pay off his debt, clean trousers—so instead of telling him more, I asked, coldly, "What other choice do you have?"

After I made sure the coast was clear (weed-puller's back to us, no other cars in sight), Sammy climbed into the backseat and we drove to Audubon Park. The smell was so bad I pinched my nose when I wasn't shifting. Sammy stayed in the car while I opened the Plymouth's trunk and found a pair of pants in the box of old clothes from which Esther had taken the jacket she made me wear to church. I had to make sure there was no sign of Stewart's Packard, or of a Chevy sedan with a cracked right headlight, or a blue Ford coupe, or anyone who looked "suspicious," before Sammy could duck walk as fast as he could to the toilets, the darkened seat of his pants hanging between his bowlegs.

I figured we'd need something for the POW to wear, so I checked to see if there was another pair of trousers. There were four more, in various sizes. I wondered why Poppa Dom had such an assortment. In the bottom of the box, wrapped in an old undershirt, I found a heavy snub-nosed pistol missing its grips. I popped it open and saw three bullets in its five chambers. It felt as if the plan had been divinely delivered, so complete and perfect were all of its details: the gun, the pants, the fact that Sammy had no choice but to lie low in the house. He'd have to do most, if not all, of the guarding since Nadine couldn't know, and he'd have no desire to slip off or share the chore since he feared Stewart and needed to hide. No longer was I worried he'd screw things up.

And then he walked out of the toilet like he didn't have a care in the world. The brown pants didn't match his drab green Air Corps uniform, but he'd cuffed them carefully, washed his face, and combed his hair. "Almost swapped clothes with an old pervert in there, but his shirt never would've fit," he said offhandedly.

I was so flabbergasted by his nonchalance that I didn't hide the gun.

"Looks like a police number," he said in his know-it-all's voice. "That'll come in handy."

Sammy was too excited to wonder why we drove around for several hours looking for a specific POW while I listened to the voice of the Florida priest droning in my head and remembered the hiss the pages made when they fell from the dictionary Andreas broke against my ear. Sammy nattered about specifics—the bets, the house on Milan—as if he'd come up with them. After I rejected yet another prisoner (guard too close, I lied) he took a deep breath, and when he spoke, his voice was less cheery. "What if we get caught?"

"We won't," I told him, and hoped we wouldn't. I put the car in gear and headed farther Uptown. For the first time I worried. What if we did? I'd thought the plan flawless but hadn't considered the many problems that could come from failure—or even from success. "You can't tell Nadine about this," I said. "You can't tell anyone."

"Sure, of course," he said, then pointed to a man too short to be Andreas who was spreading shell gravel with a rake. "How about that one?" The rest of the work gang was a hundred yards away.

"There's an old woman on the porch right there watching him," I said, and this time I wasn't making excuses. I pulled to the curb next to a small park on Annunciation. A trio of mothers kept their eyes on a trio of toddlers in a sandbox, boys playing hooky slashed each other with stick swords, a cop rode past on a motorcycle: There were more witnesses than POWs. Sammy looked bored, and I had to remind myself that I hadn't been speaking just to him when I asked what other choice there was.

Who would believe a POW when he claimed two men, one in an Army uniform, grabbed him while he was behind a hedge taking an innocent piss? Who would believe him when he recounted being held at gunpoint, driven in a rusty Plymouth to a neighborhood of small shotgun houses, hustled into one, and in its front room tied with clothesline to a brand-new kitchen chair that matched a

Formica-topped table on which there was a card that said, "Dear Benny and Macy, May You Eat Many Happy Meals Together! Mewhaw and Pawhaw"?

The German remained calm from the start, as if he'd expected to be abducted on a sunny May morning in New Orleans, just one more surprise following the surprise of surrendering in North Africa and ending up in south Louisiana.

Sammy went to park the car around the corner, and I was alone with the POW. "*Verzeih mir, Kusine,*" I said, asking forgiveness from the man whose fiancée I'd condemned.

"I have some English," he said. "I am not cousin." He kept his eyes on the gun tucked in my belt.

"*Hilf mir, Kusine,*" I begged.

For the first time he looked up from the gun. "Help you what?"

He wasn't Andreas. His quiet in the car had made me nearly sure that he was, but though his eyes were the right color, they were set too close—and his lips were too thin, his chin too weak. Only when I could study the POW's face and see he wasn't my cousin was I aware of how strongly I'd hoped Andreas had managed to follow me. It was too simple: Nadine was Ilse, Sammy was me, and I was Andreas. I wanted him to appear in New Orleans not just so I could apologize but so that I could tell him that now I knew the pain he'd felt.

"I'm sorry," I said in English.

"May I have water?" he asked.

Though I knew he wasn't Andreas, I heaved up an apology in the language my cousin and I and this unlucky prisoner shared: "I lied when you told me Ilse was pregnant, lied because I was jealous of you, had been jealous of you for years and years, so jealous that I wanted to hurt you, but my lie hurt Ilse—*killed* Ilse—and that's more hurting than I wanted to cause." I felt relief, as if I'd vomited some sour poison that'd been sloshing inside me for years, and surprise that I'd puked the confession in German: It'd been so

123

total of eighty dollars with eight bookies—eight bucks down for a payoff of $1,600. We'd agreed to split the extra $600.

I called Sammy after placing the last bet, and he gave me two more addresses. "Stewart's going to want interest," he explained, which didn't make sense since the bets I'd already made would provide a surplus, but I was pretty sure he'd been thinking, as I had, that there was no reason not to make a profit as well as save his hide. As instructed, I left two dollars with a Greek cobbler on Esplanade, but four with a bookseller in Pirate's Alley—for my troubles, a two-dollar side bet that would net me forty. I called Nadine on the bookseller's telephone to let her know I was buying her another Walter Scott novel and that I was not with Sammy. She was delighted.

I drove Uptown on Magazine with the bankers and the clerks and the lawyers and the import-export men heading home from their days behind desks on Poydras and Canal.

When I opened the front door on Milan Street, I saw first that the POW in his chair had either pitched himself or been knocked onto his side, and next that Sylvia stood beside Sammy, both of them looking down at the man who looked up at me. I closed the door and peeked out to check if anyone had seen. The street was empty and oddly quiet.

"Help me get him back up," I said. Sammy and I righted the prisoner's chair, and then I asked, "For Christ's sake, what's she doing in here?"

Sammy sighed as if fed up with my prudishness. He'd taken off the uniform jacket and rolled the sleeves of the blouse to his elbows. He wore sergeant's stripes though his jacket had captain's bars.

"I heard there was cold beer," Sylvia sassed. Her lipstick had been kissed off, and Sammy's mouth was red.

The POW coughed. "*Niemand will dir wehtun,*" I said, mainly to remind him he was to pretend he didn't speak English.

Sammy lifted his hands. "Listen, she just walked in the back door like she lived here."

"Is that when she loaned you her lipstick?"

Sylvia laughed.

"She kissed me" was his defense.

"Is anything ever your fault?" I asked.

Sylvia looked at him. Even the POW seemed to be awaiting an answer.

"Here's your gun," Sammy said, and when he passed me the pistol, it felt like a dare.

I put it in my back pocket so I wouldn't be tempted. "Did he fall over, or did you push him?"

"Fell," Sammy said.

"We came from the bedroom when we heard," Sylvia added.

I sighed at Sammy like he'd sighed at me.

Sylvia bent over the German and spoke to him brightly and slowly, as if to a three-year-old. "And what's your name?"

The POW looked at me, and I needlessly translated the question.

"Hartmut Bauer," he answered.

"I thought you called him Andreas," Sammy said to me.

I didn't remember saying my cousin's name in front of Sammy, and hearing him say it made me uneasy.

"Sylvia, when's your husband getting back?" I'd hoped to make her feel guilty, but she just smirked.

"He decided to go down to Grand Isle with the rest of them."

"He win a bet?" Sammy asked.

"Family money," she said. "From when Bobby died."

"Life insurance?" Sammy said.

"That what they call it?" Sylvia asked me.

"That's it," I agreed.

Sammy nodded, too bullheaded to figure out what she was saying.

On the way home I heard on the radio news that someone had proposed the canceled All-Star game be played in Munich, a gift for the soon-to-be victorious troops. I drove blind to the road, my eyes filled with a vision of a baseball diamond in the English Garden, a bombed and broken and burned skyline behind the outfield fence, my cousin sitting behind home plate trying to puzzle out the rules of the game. I was now convinced Andreas had never left Munich.

On Dufossat I set the brake and closed my eyes and watched a red-stitched white ball rise into my hometown's sky, heard an announcer speaking excitedly a language at once English and German.

Nadine was standing in front of the refrigerator, basking in the cold breeze. She was wearing an orange dress I hadn't seen before. Her belly was growing round again, but now a baby was the reason, not sadness. She smiled when she saw me watching from the doorway.

"Lordy, it's hot," she said. She looked into the Frigidaire. "I'm starving, Lucky Boy. What time is it?"

I looked at my watch. "Six o'clock."

"Six?" she marveled. "I was asleep in bed until about ten minutes ago," she said, patting her stomach. "It's probably too early, but I think I felt the baby move."

I was so astounded I couldn't think of anything to say except "I like that dress."

Nadine crossed her arms across her chest and tucked her chin. "It's maternity. Esther sewed it for me when I married Bobby, as a joke." Her crying sounded like hiccups. "I'm so happy, but I'm so sorry for what I did to you. How can you love me?"

She stiffened when I hugged her. "Bobby married me because I told him I was pregnant. I wasn't, but I wanted to be, and I figured I would be before he left, but I wasn't, and then he shipped out and was killed. That's the reason the Zancas hate me: After he died, they thought they'd have his child to dote on."

We stood hugging, not speaking, both of us breathing heavily. If I hadn't apologized to the POW, I would've matched her confession for confession, but I'd tried out my admission, and knew that it wouldn't balance hers; rather, the comparison would disgust her. Instead I held out the novel. "I got you this—*Waverley*."

"I swear to God I'm really pregnant now," she said. "You don't think I'm lying, do you? Because I'm not lying."

I laughed. "If this is an act, it's a good one," I said, then rubbed her belly. "We should eat something," I told her. "It'll make us feel better."

We ate breakfast at 6 p.m.: sweet rolls and café au lait.

Admitting to the POW what I'd done to Andreas opened a trapdoor in my memory, and I had to rename in English each thing I touched when the German word came to mind first—*fork, sweet roll, coffee mug, knife, butter dish, hen salt shaker, rooster pepper shaker.*

"I love you," I said, both to let her know I did, and to hear the English.

"I've never loved anyone the way I love you," she answered.

Nadine washed dishes, and I took a long bath and changed into the clean clothes she'd unpacked and put into my dresser. We sat on the couch and held hands and listened to *The Lone Ranger* and *The Thin Man,* and then Nadine unwrapped knickknacks while on a band the radio played rumbas in Miami.

"Is this important?" she asked. It was the envelope I'd used to record and then decipher the Morse code I'd heard at the movies and that'd rattled in my head off and on since the day I'd been fired. It still held the peacock shape of the salt shaker that'd been wrapped in it. *Hilfmirkusine* was penciled in my handwriting. I'd so badly wanted the POW to be Andreas that my memory had scrambled the newsreel's noise into a message from my cousin, or for him. I was amazed, but I held a calm face.

"That's trash," I told her.

She crushed it into a ball and held the wadded envelope in one